WHAT MEETS THE EYE?
THE DEAF PERSPECTIVE

Edited by
Lisa Kelly and Sophie Stone

ARACHNE PRESS

First published in UK 2021 by Arachne Press Limited
100 Grierson Road, London SE23 1NX
www.arachnepress.com
© Arachne Press 2021
ISBNs
Print 978-1-913665-48-7
eBook 978-1-913665-49-4

These poems and stories are also available in BSL on the Arachne Press website: arachnepress.com

The moral rights of the authors have been asserted.
Detailed copyright on page 3.

All rights reserved. This book is sold subject to the condition that it shall not by way of trade or otherwise, be lent, resold, hired out or otherwise circulated without the publisher's prior written consent in any form or binding or cover other than that in which it is published and without similar condition including this condition being imposed on the subsequent purchaser.

Except for short passages for review purposes no part of this publication may be reproduced, stored in a retrieval system or transmitted in any form, or by any means, electronic, mechanical, photocopying, recording or otherwise without prior written permission of Arachne Press Limited.

Thanks to Muireann Grealy for her proofing.
Thanks to Nina Thomas for her cover design.

Printed on wood-free paper in the UK by TJ Books, Padstow.

The publication of this book is supported using public funding by the National Lottery through Arts Council England.

Acknowledgements

Introduction © Lisa Kelly & Sophie Stone 2021
Preface © Raymond Antrobus 2021
A Map towards Fluency (first published Carcanet Press 2019 reprinted with their permission) and *Ear Trumpet* first published zoeglossia 2021 © Lisa Kelly
A Word of Warning and *Pushing Boundaries* © Clare-Louise English 2021
After Stagnation © Melanie Ashford 2021
After the Row and *Paper Bags Always Meant One Thing* © Alison Campbell 2021
Ailbhe's Tale © Lynn Buckle 2021 commissioned by The National Centre for Writing
Bones Under Their Feet and *La Favorite* © Josephine Dickinson 2021
Circus of Change © Ksenia Balabina 2021
Coastal Walking for the Hard of Hearing © David Callin 2021
Coffee Shop © Colly Metcalfe 2021
de Belder Guido © Rodney Wood 2021
Deaf Rights, The Dancer and *The Silent Linguist* © Sarah O Adedeji 2021
DeLorean © Charlie Swinbourne 2021
De-stiffen © Dee Cooke 2021
Dream Catcher and *Sea Pool* © Marilyn Longstaff 2021
First as Body, then as Metaphor © Khando Langri 2021
Fish and the Blue-Arsed Fly and *In Two Minds* © Julie Boden 2021
Growing Pains and *Loops* © Elizabeth Ward 2021
I Will Talk For You © Maryam Ebrahim 2021
I , Nyx: (A Daughter's Daughter) © Sophie Stone 2021
In Memory of our Father and *Sense of Direction* © Ayesha B Gavin 2021
Label © Mary-Jayne Russell de Clifford 2021
Lockdown Lyric © John Kefala Kerr 2021
MAPping a New Landscape © DL Williams 2021
Moving Words © Bryony Parkes 2021
My Glow © Sahera Khan 2021
Neutral © Sophie Woolley 2021. Originally developed with support from Hot Coals Productions
No Return – Move On and *Now* © Maggie Arbeid 2021
One or Two Interesting Facts about Dad and *With My Back to the Wall*

© Janet Hatherley 2021
Quiet Twosome © Samantha Baines 2021
The Cycle (Of Important Nothings) © Terri Donovan 2021
The Dice Players © John Wilson 2021
The Home Secretary Doth Protest Too Much © Liam O'Dell 2021
This is Not a Race © Sarah Clarke 2021
Thursday 7th November 2019 and *Why Can't You Learn Sign Language?*
© Lianne Herbert 2021
Tracking Sounds, Crossing Borders © Emma Lee 2021
Wagging the Dog © Jay Caldwell 2021
Walking is an Option © Diane Dobson 2021
Where is Syria? © Hala Hashem 2021

Quotations from *Elegy in Translation* by Meg Day, by kind permission of the author.

Quotations from *Diary of a Newly Wed Poet, To Cadiz on the Train January 28th, Ideal Arrival, New York Night* and *Time and Space*, from *The Poet and the Sea*, by Juan Ramón Jiménez translated by Mary Berg and Dennis Maloney, White Pine Press, by kind permission of the publishers.

Quotation from *I Am Not I* from *Lorca & Jimenez: Selected Poems* by Robert Bly, Beacon Press, by kind permission of the publishers.

WHAT MEETS THE EYE?
THE DEAF PERSPECTIVE

Contents

Introduction	Lisa Kelly & Sophie Stone	9
Preface	Raymond Antrobus	11
Growing Pains	Elizabeth Ward	23
Label	Mary-Jayne Russell de Clifford	24
Tracking Sounds Crossing Borders	Emma Lee	26
Thursday 7th November 2019	Lianne Herbert	28
No Return – Move On	Maggie Arbeid	30
Lockdown Lyric	John Kefala Kerr	31
After Stagnation	Melanie Ashford	36
Now	Maggie Arbeid	37
MAPping a New Landscape	DL Williams	38
Neutral	Sophie Woolley	40
After the Row	Alison Campbell	58
Circus of Change	Ksenia Balabina	60
Coastal Walking for the Hard of Hearing	David Callin	62
Walking is an Option	Diane Dobson	63
A Word of Warning	Clare-Louise English	68
Quiet Twosome	Samantha Baines	69
Wagging the Dog	Jay Caldwell	70
de Belder Guido	Rodney Wood	72
A Map towards Fluency	Lisa Kelly	73
Loops	Elizabeth Ward	77
Coffee Shop	Colly Metcalfe	78
Paper Bags Always Meant One Thing	Alison Campbell	83
Fish and the Blue-Arsed Fly	Julie Boden	84

Sea Pool	Marilyn Longstaff	85
Ailbhe's Tale	Lynn Buckle	86
Bones Under Their Feet	Josephine Dickinson	92
DeLorean	Charlie Swinbourne	95
Sense of Direction	Ayesha B Gavin	97
Where is Syria	Hala Hashem	99
In Memory of our Father	Ayesha B Gavin	101
One or Two Interesting Facts about Dad	Janet Hatherley	103
With My Back to the Wall	Janet Hatherley	104
I, Nyx: (A Daughter's Daughter)	Sophie Stone	104
My Glow	Sahera Khan	109
Ear Trumpet	Lisa Kelly	112
Moving Words	Bryony Parkes	113
Deaf Rights	Sarah O Adedeji	117
The Home Secretary Doth Protest Too Much	Liam O'Dell	118
Pushing Boundaries	Clare-Louise English	119
The Dice Players	John Wilson	121
I Will Talk For You	Maryam Ebrahim	127
Why Can't You Learn Sign Language?	Lianne Herbert	128
The Dancer	Sarah O Adedeji	130
The Silent Linguist	Sarah O Adedeji	132
Dream Catcher	Marilyn Longstaff	135
In Two Minds	Julie Boden	136
De-stiffen	Dee Cooke	138
This is Not a Race	Sarah Clarke	139
La Favorite	Josephine Dickinson	143

The Cycle (Of Important Nothings)	Terri Donovan	145
First as Body, then as Metaphor	Khando Langri	148

Link to BSL Videos
by the authors, and translators

Introduction
Lisa Kelly and Sophie Stone

Welcome to *What Meets the Eye*, an anthology that aims to share a multitude of journeys exploring Deaf, deaf and Hard of Hearing experiences by British writers. If you are looking for a definitive take on deafness, you must look for another anthology; however, if you are looking to join us venturing in exciting and varied territories where mountains of prejudice must be climbed, emotional currents swum, and landmarks reached that lend breath-taking perspectives on what it means to be Deaf, deaf or Hard of Hearing, then you will meet us eye to eye.

This book is part of a series of anthologies produced by Arachne Press loosely linked to a theme of *Maps and Mapping*, and we took our theme, *Movement*, from that. When we first discussed putting together this anthology, we knew we wanted wide horizons, not circumscribed by a single vision of form, style or voice – just as deafness is not circumscribed by a single identity, attitude, or political stance. You will meet writers you recognise, writers you are not familiar with, and writers who you will want to search out in other ventures. The one consistent part of the journey is access. From the beginning we decided that however we received work – in British Sign Language (BSL) or English – it should be translated and accessible in both languages (follow the link after the contents or at the end of this book for the BSL version).

As a Deaf, deaf or Hard of Hearing writer, the only certainty is movement. Society, politics, medicine, access, ageing and culture all continue to shape our landscape. How change is navigated lends itself to the richest experiences, which in turn lend themselves to the richest literary expressions. Working with and around the dominance of the hearing world and English speakers, where BSL does not yet have any legal status, unlike the Welsh, Gaelic, and Cornish languages, inevitably gives this anthology a political heart, of which we are proud, and we hope it inspires further activism. At the time of writing, a judge has ruled the UK government broke the Equality Act 2010, by failing to provide a BSL interpreter for its scientific briefings on the coronavirus. The victory followed a campaign led by Deaf activists, *#WhereIsTheInterpreter*, and shows how much can be achieved through collective action. Individual responses to discrimination, prejudice, and societal injustice, however, will find outlet in artistic expression as each journey is negotiated. We hope you will be moved by how our authors have interpreted the theme of movement. If you are Deaf, deaf or Hard of Hearing, we hope you are moved to consider your own journey and perhaps be inspired to write about your experiences and share writing that connects with you. If you are hearing, we hope you are moved to shared understandings and a broader perspective on what it means to be Deaf, deaf or Hard of Hearing where the hearing culture is dominant. Above all we hope you are entertained by your journey through *What Meets the Eye* and let your experience move through you and beyond you to reach even wider audiences. This is just the beginning.

Preface
Raymond Antrobus

19th February 2021
My wife Tabitha and I visit a midwifery community centre in Oklahoma. She is ten weeks pregnant. We find ourselves in a room with light green walls with portraits of young mothers smiling into the eyes of newborn babies. We sit on the sofa, I place the cushion on my lap instead of sitting on it, perhaps a sign that I am unwilling to get too comfortable, and yet we are filled with the excitement and anxiety of most expectant parents. I can smell my coffee breath trapped behind my mask, the windowless room has a thick air-conditioned heat and relies on the florescent light in a way that makes the room feel artificial, like an eye that doesn't blink. It is a pandemic and the midwife in the room with us isn't wearing a mask so Tabitha and I are already unnerved. When she leaves the room I happen to pick up a leaflet about hearing tests for newborn babies. A trigger warning about ableist language, the leaflet explains how children born with 'hearing loss' socially and academically lag behind their hearing peers. It goes on for two pages about language acquisition in the first seven years of a child's life and the 'challenges the child will face with hearing loss'; nowhere in the literature does it mention deaf awareness, sign language or the culturally Deaf. I'm not denying there are challenges but pathologising a child's deafness instead of society's ableism is a cruel oversight. I don't keep the pamphlet. I am too angry. I put it back and Tabitha and I leave the building.

That whole week I had been doing readings of my first children's picture book *Can Bears Ski?* a story based on my own experience growing up hard of hearing with hearing parents who struggled to guide me through the hearing world. Part of the purpose of the story is to show deafness as an experience rather than a trauma.

I got a range of questions from deaf young readers, some engaged with the story, asking 'Why does the moon have a face?' And 'Can the bears sign?', and there were young readers looking at the other faces on the zoom call and asking 'How many people here have cochlear implants?'; another question was 'Does anyone here have red hearing aids?', but a common question was 'What is good about being deaf?'. There is an innocence to this question, but there's also a self-consciousness, one that some would say ought to not exist for children so young, but alas, from birth we're lucky to be born in a room that isn't ableist, let alone a world.

What does this mean to the poet? What is our role, how can we engage and challenge the norms of ableist practice? While browsing in the London Library, I came across the work of John Kitto, a profoundly deaf poet and English Bible scholar born in England. In 1845 Kitto published *The Lost Senses: Deafness And Blindness*. A fascinating read, Kitto includes a selection of his own sonnets and offers commentary on their inferiority to Shakespeare. He blames his inferiority on his deafness, and in tight iambic pentameter mourns his deafness. As graceful as his writing is, it is still internalised ableism. I don't mean to say this has no place in literature, it is real, but it is something to notice and interrogate when, and if, it shows up in our own work and our own words, as poets with disabilities. I'm not a scholar, if I were I'd have saved all my notes from the days I spent reading John Kitto. His poems certainly inspired me to develop my own deaf poetics, a lyricism that is at once personal and specific to my experience of deafness, but one that is also subjective and rich. My first full collection, *The Perseverance*, does this by leaning into the forms of repetition. Much of my experience in the hearing world is asking people to repeat themselves; this is defiance, this is also vigilance.

10th March 2021

Being vigilant in our reading as poets may pay off in our writing as poets, so I want to talk briefly about the Spanish poet Juan Ramón Jiménez and how his work helped me make some decisions in my own writing. I'm a non-Spanish speaker, so the English language translators I've relied on are Robert Bly, Mary G Berg and Dennis Maloney.

On 16th January 1916, Jiménez was in his early thirties, already an accomplished poet, prose writer and children's author. He was leaving on a train from Madrid to board a boat at the port of Cadiz, sailing on to New York where he was due to marry.

He begins a poem in his diary,

> *How close now to my soul,*
> *What still seems so very far*
> *From my hands!*

Jiménez was in love, a young poet in full visceral yearning mode, a poet influenced by the lyric intensity of Rilke and the French Symbolism of Rimbaud. On his sea crossing Jiménez would write some of the most revered poems in Spanish literature. Each of the poems would be dated between 16th January - 3rd October. Some of the poems read like the fragmented internal dialogue of a mystic drifting off to sleep. In Jiménez's imagination, any boundary between land, sky and sea melts away and we readers find ourselves in the world where colour itself is a kind of destination.

...the train doesn't go toward the sea ponders the speaker, in a short poem addressed *To Cadiz on the Train, January 28th*, the

line runs on, *it goes toward the green summer of gold and white.*
Yellow and *green* dominate so much of Jiménez's metaphysical imagery that the colours become synonymous with his name. Just over a hundred years after Jiménez took his trip, married and published the poems that became *Diary of a Newly Wed Poet*, I find myself in my early thirties, having written a poetry collection and a children's picture book. I've just finished a long journey by train to Heathrow where I catch my flight to JFK. I am in a long-distance relationship and am engaged and soon to marry in America. From JFK airport I take a cab to Queens, Ridgewood, and some lines for a poem come to me, which I draft in my notebook:

> *Give thanks, the wheel touching tarmac at JFK,*
> *Give thanks, the latches, handles, what we squeeze*
>
> *into cabins, the wobbling wings, the arrivals,*
> *departures, long line at the gates, the held nerve...*
>
> *the give / of rain on the windows*

Each line is a runway, the alliterated lines *touching tarmac* and *wobbling wings* create the energetic physical quality of taking off, and the enjambed run on lines keep the reader guessing where the poem may land.

In the sky, I'm a nervous flyer, and on the ground I usually get stopped, searched and questioned at airports, but on this particular trip I've gotten past the border swiftly. (It may have had something to do with the fact that I am wearing a suit and tie like the one that Jiménez bears on the cover of the 1916 first edition of *Diary Of A Newly Wed Poet*).

I haven't yet read *Diary of a Newly Wed Poet*, I am a year away from finding Robert Bly's translation of it in a second-hand bookshop, a year away from resonating with the lines *I will leap over the sea / through the sky / I will go far, so very far / that my body won't remember your body / or mine!*

The poem I drafted after landing in JFK is now the opening (untitled) poem of my poetry book *All The Names Given* (Picador). I'd thought I'd finished writing *All The Names Given* when I learned of Jiménez, but once I'd felt inspired by *Diary of A Newly Wed Poet* I rushed back to the manuscript to make tweaks with Jiménez as a literary touchstone or better yet, a kind of poetic time-travelling companion.

16th March 2020
I Am Not I by Jiménez
Translator, Robert Bly

> *I am not I.*
>   *I am this one*
> *walking beside me whom I do not see,*
> *whom at times I manage to visit,*
> *and whom at other times I forget;*
> *who remains calm and silent while I talk,*
> *and forgives, gently, when I hate,*
> *who walks where I am not,*
> *who will remain standing when I die.*

Today I was mentoring a young poet on Zoom who said she didn't like contemporary poetry, she found it too 'political' and 'identity based'. In her words, she much preferred the 'more abstract and visceral poets of the 19th century'. She reeled off a list of mostly straight middle-class white women poets (Emily Dickinson, Christina Rossetti, Elizabeth Barrett Browning). She liked that these poets had 'quiet' and 'private voices', they wrote in rhyme and strict metered lines, they were remnants of old times, legacy-managed and glorified (by no fault of their own) as pure poets. Somehow their work wasn't 'political' or 'identity based'. I'd heard Ilya Kaminsky once say that this seems to be a phenomenon in America and the UK, the idea of 'political poetry' as a standalone genre, *everywhere else in the world, what gets called political poetry is just poetry everywhere else* says Kaminsky.

I do agree, that with the visceral nature of some poetry, the air and open-endedness can widen its relatability. Poetry is certainly worthwhile when we are able to pursue our own thoughts through it, despite the separate reaches of space, time (and identity) of the reader and the poet.

Juan Ramón Jiménez wrote his last book in 1958, a poetic autobiography called *Time and Space*. He writes, *Poetry comes to me as an answer, made up from the very essence of my questions.*

Jiménez spent much of his life in political exile. His roaming opened up his earthly questions of citizenship and ethereal questions of mind, body, time and space. In a poem titled *The Sea*, written on 10th October 1916, after months sailing the Atlantic heading to America, he wrote *any moment the sea / can be almost human in order to hate me. / It doesn't know who I am.* The weather, the environment, all have their own human and *almost human* identities.

Now, as poets with disabilities, how do we respond to these identity questions? Is there a school of thought that says we ought to hide these earthly elements of who we are in pursuit of the transcendental? The lyric so high that it leaves the body on earth altogether? What are our questions? How do we interrogate this in our own practice?

Of course, going back to the student, what she seems to be unconsciously expressing is a kind of toxic nostalgia for the good old days when the only poets worth knowing about just so happened to be abled-bodied, white and middle class. I tried tactfully to point this out to the young poet, but I'm not always the best at managing my own neurosis and my tone can come across as defensive, which doesn't help anything. So, my question is, why was this poet so resistant to expanding her references and project? Is it white guilt? Is it white fear of becoming irrelevant after centuries of default status? Is it just the stubborn naivety of a young poet and nothing more?

I asked what she knew about contemporary women poets? I suggested Eavan Boland, Lucille Clifton, Adrienne Rich and June Jordan as entry points; then, if she was looking for contemporary women poets that have achieved new kinds of lyrical language and ways of seeing, then she ought to read Layli Long Soldier, Solmaz Sharif and Valzhyna Mort, but the young poet sounded doubtful: 'these poets sound too political and that's not what I'm trying to do'. A version of this discussion exists in almost every academic space I've taught in (most of which are in the UK) and a lot of literature students are still being educated with this toxic nostalgia, this so-called unidentifiable whiteness. As populist as James Baldwin and Audre Lorde have become with progressive thinkers and activists, their arguments and perspectives don't seem to be common practice in institutions – despite each of these institutions releasing Black Lives Matter statements in the wake of George Floyd.

Of course, I recognize this poet has a specific interest in 19th century women poets, but she must realise that her taste is political and identity-based, and that is ok, that is as human as the child I saw in my online reading last week, looking through his screen asking, 'Does anyone here have red hearing aids?'

17th March 2021

Forgive me my deafness now for your name on others' lips: begins Deaf poet Meg Day's lyrical and intimate poem, *Elegy in Translation*. You'd be forgiven for wondering how this poem is an *elegy* – it doesn't mention a literal death, but hints at a symbolic death. Perhaps the speaker is lamenting the death of a former self, one that was ashamed of their deafness, as the speaker asks us again, later in the poem, *Forgive me / my deafness for my own sound, how I mistook it for a wound / you could heal.* I resonated with this idea of having your own sound. Have you ever been in a room when someone asked, 'Can you hear that?' and only had a blank face to give? Were you ever in those English classes where you're taught how to write iambic pentameter? Taught it as if it is the sole measure of sound and poetic value? Did you almost weep when you read Kamau Braithwaite's line *the hurricane does not roar in pentameters?* Did you resonate with that line so fiercely you slammed your fist on the table in the study area of the library, immediately being shushed by the librarian? There are many layers to one's 'own sound', it hints at a need to nurture a poetic sensibility, a kind of personal music in the noisy world of language. Speaking of music, a memorable line of this poem goes, *So what / if Johnny Nash can see clearly now Lorraine is gone—I only wanted / to hear the sea.*

Mishearings are an obvious staple of deaf poetics, of course, a way to honour one's own sound – *Lorraine* being a corruption of *the rain.* Even knowing that Meg Day is an American poet and happens to be listening to Johnny Nash's version of the song tells us something significant (I'm more familiar with Jimmy Cliff's cover). This poem also engages with the physicality of sign language and perhaps this is one of the places where the idea of 'translation' comes into the poem. The speaker uses some of the semantics that those familiar with the Deaf community will understand, for example, when the speaker says *My hands are bloated / with the name signs of my kin.* In the Deaf world, friends have sign names that can only be assigned to you by someone else in the Deaf community.

Despite this specificity it's not something that alienates anyone because whether you are clued into Deaf culture or not, the verb *bloated* is active enough in multiple ways with *name signs*, which works as both a concrete and an abstract noun. These kinds of linguistic gymnastics and poetic devices are woven throughout the poem, using slant and internal rhymes and alliteration, techniques hard to pull off meaningfully, and contrast with the image near the beginning of the *fluke of tongues*. The poetic accomplishment here is far from fluke, it's an intentional affirmation of one's own sound, it's a tongue in cheek lament, it's skilled and measured, written by a Deaf poet at the height of their powers.

I'd like to contrast Meg Day's *Elegy in Translation* with the 18th century poet, botanist and preacher John Kitto's *Alternatives*, published in 1884.

> *Were all the beams that ever shone,*
> *From all the stars of day and night,*
> *Collected in one single cone,*
>   *Unutterably bright!*
> *I'd give them for one glance of heaven*
> *Which might but hint of sin forgiven.*
>
> *Could all the voices and glad sounds*
> *Which have not fallen on my sense,*
> *Be rendered up in one hour's bounds,*
>   *A gift immense,*
> *I'd for one whisper to my heart*
> *Give all the joy this might impart.*
>
> *If the great deep now offered all*
> *The treasures in her bosom stored,*
> *And at my feet I could now call*

> *That might hoard,*
> *I'd spurn it utterly for some*
> *Small treasure in the world to come.*
>
> *If the sweet scents of every flower—*
> *Each one of which cheers more than wine—*
> *One plant could from its petals pour,*
> *   And that were mine,*
> *I would give up that glorious prize*
> *For one faint breath from Paradise.*
>
> *Were all the pleasures I have known,*
> *'So far, so very far between',*
> *Into one great sensation thrown –*
> *   Not then all mean—*
> *I'd give it freely for one smile*
> *From Him who died for me erewhile.*

Derek Walcott once said that he has *never separated the writing of poetry from prayer.* This poem may show readers how they can be one and the same. The line length and rhythm may put readers in the mind of *In The Bleak Midwinter* by Christina Rossetti, which was published as a poem before becoming popularised as a hymn. If a famous composer found Kitto's poem, my hunch is it too would have been popularised as a hymn, but instead it's been lost to history, tucked into a book I would happen to find two centuries later in the miscellaneous section on the Deaf shelf of the London Library. I was moved by this poem when I first read it. I leaned back and smiled. It demands multiple readings (out loud) but initially the ecstatic images from the implied light of the stars, moon and sun, to heaven and the flowers bring this poem to brightness. There is a rhyme scheme (AB AB CC) which allows each stanza to circle the sound of its themes, which I like to think of as divinity, sound, nature and disability. Reading this poem more deeply it struck on another level, that perhaps this is a queer poem about forbidden love shrouded in religious sentiment? It feels particularly erotic in the last stanza with the mention of pleasures, sensation and giving for one smile From Him. Also thinking of how that joins with the end of the first stanza, *I'd give them for one glance of heaven/ Which might but hint of sin forgiven.*

Here we have two poems that mention forgiveness. There is an intimacy in both poems as well as transcendence, and yet both poems take different approaches to similar ideas. There is a journey towards growth, self-affirmation and acceptance; there is an earned ability, centuries apart, to sing one's own sound.

18th March 2021

Let me circle back to Jiménez and his 1916 voyage in which he wrote *Diary of a Newly Wed Poet*. The way I have described his poetry so far could be assumed to be high lyric, raceless, genderless, classless, amoral transcendentalism. Jiménez does in fact mention race and class in numerous poems. He notices fellow travellers on the ship, in the prose poem *Ideal Arrival* where all races *Blacks, whites, Asians* become *brothers in their happiness*, perhaps a naive or sarcastic observation? Or perhaps a kinship with marginalised people? In another poem, *New York Night*, Jiménez describes *the poor people who live here/ Chinese, Irish, Jewish, Black/ stirred into one wretched dream/ all their nightmares of hunger*. My interpretation is that, as a traveller, Jiménez has found some kind of equality; we are all at the mercy of the sea and the sky, and yet Jiménez does have moments of Buddhist generosity: *I stepped one afternoon/ into other rooms... as much mine as the world*.

Sweeping lines like this can be received well by many kinds of readers when we see (elsewhere in Jiménez's poems) that his sociological gaze is beyond himself – that he isn't whitewashing the world around him, or denying ways of living outside of his own understanding, that he acknowledges the world while decentring himself. In *Time and Space*, he writes *Nature looks at me like an alien thing, the flower, the flight, the bad smells, the mosquitoes... infinite harmony, the whole melody of which I am only one note.*

Maybe I'm wrong and these are my biases? Jiménez may be using feminine or masculine language in ways that aren't progressive. I might be glorifying his poetry because of how much of it aligns with my own ideals and experience. This isn't a problem in and of itself, but I do think we ought to be aware of our biases, in case we end up perpetuating reductive ideas that in turn shut down discussion and exploration into our own experiences, as well as others.

So I want to encourage wide and fearless reading and learning, and I want to celebrate the poets that allow us a kind of *permanent arrival* as Jiménez put it, at our own shores and beyond.

Writers, go forth. Have your adventures, ask your questions and stay vigilant.

Elizabeth Ward
Growing Pains

In the dark, I go digging—
for the roots, the beginning:

in the fertile soil of my mind,
the half-moon is shining

alighting on hidden recesses—
on soil-stained unfurling fingers

life of burnt longing, lit with memory,
blank open page scrawled with mud

in the green bud of frosted spring,
let me assuage the grief I carry:

—buried in the roots, the soil, the damp—

I turn this vernal earth with blunted shovel.

Mary-Jayne Russell de Clifford
Label

I am Deaf, me.
This is my identity.
I discovered University,
His eyes discovered me.
Our eyes danced
My 'I' became 'Us'
'Girlfriend'
Graduated
to 'Mother'
(hesitantly).
A son grew inside of me
I took marriage, morality.
Moved by maternity
but our 'us'
struggled
wrestled
parted.
I held my son
I am a single mum to a
Neurodiverse child.
His father returns to divorce me.
I hunt for love and
I find her
but soon I'm the hunted
the prey
she claws at my mind
and I crumble inside.

I break free
re-assess my sexuality.
The damage I see all around makes
a defiantly Vegan me.
I seek faith, spirituality
the Bible and God comes to me
fellowship, a community –
till their judging eyes lay labels upon me
I felt the impurity –
I left and was free.
I didn't feel I belonged
anywhere.
I
alone
lonely.
Who is this 'I'?

I am here.
I reject your labels.
Life moves and
I with it.

Emma Lee
Tracking Sounds, Crossing Borders

I watch the stylus track the groove in the record
and the flicker on the amplifier as Ella sings.
My mother and grandmother talk as if I'm not
in the room. Yesterday in class, the teacher
watched me. Her mouth was closed. I'd finished
the work on the board, was doing nothing wrong.
I felt Claire's elbow and turned. Her mouth said
she'd called my name. My mother's all elbows
and angles, her smile doesn't reach her eyes.
I watched the trees wave green leaves. It wasn't
until after my operation I discovered that brown
leaves rustle when the breeze makes them dance.

Who knew snow crunched? I could hear the rhythms
of someone's speech, but not the tone. I watched
expressions and body language to compensate.
When I read my poems to an audience I look for
a smile of recognition, the stillness of true listening,
a fidget of boredom, a clue into how I'm heard.
Discussing students reading aloud with my teenager,
she mentioned she imagines me reading them.
Looked puzzled when I said I only hear in monotone.

In the cafe bar, I sit at the spare table. I need several
moments to filter the background chatter, the clatter,
the coffee machine and I know music is playing.
But plastic chairs, aluminium tables, hard floor
and walls, echo along with the tinnitus in my ears.
When I buy a coffee, I lip read. I tick
'prefer not to say' on forms. I can pass, get by.
I feel the dig of Claire's elbow, the teacher watching,
my mother saying *failure* and I still haven't worked out
where the border between hard of hearing and deaf lies.

Lianne Herbert
Thursday 7th November 2019

i wanted to tell you i was hurting
whilst asking about your deleted social media.
i didn't expect you to answer.
i fell asleep. i couldn't take anymore.
you replied social media is 'too much'.
but i needed someone to talk to.
'i feel like i have no one to talk to'.
how fucking true that was.
i needed a hug from you, even though we ain't close.
check on me more often, yeah?
whilst dad read bedtime stories to my son
i took some baileys over ice with three zopiclone as a cry for help
'no!' my dead nanna's spirit screams.
'i'm sorry' i messaged my mum.
texted 999. ambulance came.
shocked my dad and brother when at the door.
it was a cold night, went to a&e for seven hours.
i wanted to tell you 'i'm still alive'.

i *wanted* to tell you 'i'm *still* alive'.
it was a cold night, went to a&e for seven hours.
shocked my dad and brother when at the door.
texted 999. ambulance came.
'i'm sorry' i messaged my mum.
'*no!*' my dead nanna's spirit screams.
i took some baileys over ice with three zopiclone as a cry for help
whilst dad read bedtime stories to my son.
check on me more often, *yeah?*
i needed a hug from you, even though we ain't close.
how *fucking true* that was —
'i feel like i have no one to talk to'.
but i *needed* someone to talk to.
you replied social media is 'too much'.
i fell asleep. i couldn't take anymore.
i didn't expect you to answer.
whilst asking about your deleted social media
i *wanted* to tell you i was *hurting*.

Maggie Arbeid
No Return – Move On

Slipping down the slope
to inertia – sloth and apathy
to some sort of revival and purpose –
on my own – no longer able to avoid
the technological age – the world second-hand.

My patient friend says:
It really is quite easy, just try, just play,
look to the future online.
But where is the energy, the interest,
the will to carry me along to –
a new way of being?

My brain drained –
this foreign place – a new language
to understand, new values to live by
and connect with – old values gone –
old enthusiasms, which drove me creatively –
galleries, theatres, concerts –
music communicated live – now –
a second-hand experience – on a screen –
isolated and controlled – no pleasure shared.

Shopping online, no senses used, no touching,
no feeling, no perfume-trying – just branding.
A shopping trip with a friend – an adventure,
a chat over coffee and cake, city centre – all gone
in shut down – vibrant Brighton by the sea –
waiting to be washed away.

John Kefala Kerr
Lockdown Lyric

I
out of milk, we hit the back lanes
(there are zombies about!)

a discarded heater lies on its back
so many others like that Bowie would say

we have almond milk but it curdles
I drink it anyway, recalling my nightmare:

sabotaged elevator, trapped occupants,
lockdown handle, desperate bid to escape.

you are the perfect companion (a Darling Bud)
your instincts frugal... no, opulent—

grocery slots appear at midnight
the supermarket Santa wears green

DME stands for 'distance measuring equipment'
the calibration in tenths of a mile—

OK for planes but too crude for pandemics—
our eyes identify targets and our legs respond:

avoid the huge dog, the roundabout,
Marie Celeste buses, magpies on pavements

at dusk, the electric star is underlined
by a chalky stripe from a rare high flyer;

the vapour drifts, deserting the star,
draping the moon in a gauzy chemise

the birds' evensong is balloon-twist magic,
a sweep across the AM dial

today we went out in our thin shoes
and you said it was like walking in slippers

the next day I said:
do you remember us going out in our thin shoes?
and you said:
yes, they were very thin.

II
what are those trolleys called that you push?
the woman at the clinic had one

examining the zip – she says, *it goes
this way, but I'm right-handed!*

I respond with lockdown fads—
new guitar strings, fixing bikes...

test rides happen in the back lane
with the SUV guys revving up

Captain Tom had a trolley,
but the SUV guys have real power

they demonstrate it, on hire,
via Audi, Mercedes, BMW

the junkies are out early
(emergency rendezvous)

some people wear masks
but we prefer to zig-zag

between the Corner of Death
and the Phone Box of Birth

III
this can't be my neighbourhood
what a lovely place!

hello sky, hello air, hello England
goodbye... other things

see the hedges of the deprived
clipped close to topiary

and the ornamental
Dyson posing for my lens?

I want to write songs again
be a teenage bard—

Land of Epidemiology
(my biggest hit),
The Risks of Unfettered Capitalism
(the B-side)

we listen to the squeaky-wheel bird
before boarding our boat (the sofa),

which floats on a sea of laminate,
and drink tea after sleep…

pondering our next move,
we save *Scotland from Above* for later

and ride out to the contaminated beach
to see the duck

IV
we pushed the boat out today
far enough to conjure a marina

and equate the dinghy there
to alfresco sausages and beer

we pedalled a teardrop route,
avoidance looming large

and drinkable things piling up
—milk, beer, detergent…

V
at night people can't breathe
and this is the real evacuation

that VE Day can't swallow
in this smash-and-grab war

for air (the pinched prize)
where the pressure drops

and the tube in the mouth
and the pipe in the throat

make now a time of panic
of agents of medicine

attending to ditched vessels
and cries for a scuba team

and faces behind screens
bringing gusts of love

—all entirely breathable
though not by lungs

Melanie Ashford
After Stagnation

The Blast!
The liberty!
You suffocate

on the freedom.

The tears
flow from your eyes,
as you begin to take steps

after years of entrapment.

You choke on
the oxygen, or is it the relief,
of finally being granted the liberty

falsely taken from you.

And the air,
oh! the air!
The air is like nectar,

dripping into your lungs.

Maggie Arbeid
Now

Now I feel my life
has no commas or full stops
no form nor structure
I am wandering among
my chaos buried in detail
trying to enjoy the spaces
in between

DL Williams
MAPping a New Landscape

A new map is being drawn.
With each new sound
another shade appears.
New countries,
entire new continents
rise from the abyss.

Long lost lands,
previously unreachable.
Probing signals
receiving 'no response'
and tissues for the tears.

Now rediscovered,
this unfamiliar terrain
is charted by screens and wires.
New lines are sketched,
valleys and peaks
are graphed and defined.

This territory of noise,
comfort levels
and threshold limits
denote the boundaries
of acoustic tolerance.

Here be monsters.
Beware the cackling
crackling crisp packets
seeking the last crisp.
Forfend the blaring, waffling,
singing, chattering TV adverts.

Be brave
when birds are tweeting,
chirruping themselves silly.
Be on guard for ambushes
by random, unexpected reports.

A new map is being drawn.
Long lost lands
now rediscovered,
this territory of noise.
Here be monsters.
Be brave.

MAPping, or mapping, is when a new program is created for a cochlear implant based on the user's audiogram and by testing their C-levels and T-levels – comfort levels and threshold limits – with hearing tests while using the CI.

Sophie Woolley
Neutral

> Notes on formats:
> Spoken English is in plain text.
> **BSL is in bold.**
> *Italics for actions.*
> CAPITALS FOR TEXT OF SAF'S GOOGLING
> as it would appear, superimposed on screen (not as part of the subtitles)

PROLOGUE

In a caravan, in between the sofa table and the kitchen area, SAF is dancing to music bluetoothed direct to her cochlear implant processor. She looks into a mirror and puts on a stylish bucket hat, admiring her reflection.

SAF
(Big Brother narrator style)
Day two in the caravan. Saf is dancing to music only she can hear. A facemask hangs from one ear.
(She silently mouths the lyrics of a Sylvia Striplin song, 'You Can't Turn me Away'.) She moves to the music confidently. We are not here.
You can't turn me away.

She grooves. She sees someone outside the window. She stops and nods to the unseen person.
(Shouting to person outside the caravan)
Just getting my wellies on. And my mask.
Saf puts on her wellington boots. She looks in the mirror, takes a mirror selfie. Tells herself:

I'll be back.

Looking in the mirror, she sees us and playfully 'shoots' us with her fingers, like a Charlie's Angel publicity shot. She pauses and speaks to us directly, via the mirror, replying as if we gave her a 'whaaaaat?' look.

What?! I'm on holiday.

> *(Big Brother narrator style)*
> Day two in the caravan and Saf is going to the actual pub!

Saf puts her mask on and exits the caravan.

PART 1

Saf enters caravan wearing a facemask and jacket, her hair and clothes slightly wet from the rain. She puts down the umbrella, awkwardly takes her shoes off on the mat, being careful not to muddy the caravan floor.

SAF
(Under her breath)

Just take these off...*(sighs)* covered in mud. Got to try and keep the caravan super clean, because this is Steph's. She's just arriving back now. Hi...

Saf waves out the window, thumbs up. She sits and looks and sighs at us as if to say, 'sorry about the wait'. She unhooks one side of the facemask, leaving it dangling from the other ear, as per the new normal for her. She disinfects her hands.

(Under her breath)

Just do my hands.

(Speaking at usual volume level)

I walked back from the pub early, got caught in the rain... I don't mind the rain actually. Or the pandemic. Makes me feel alive. I'm good at adapting to rubbishness. It's a deaf skill. **Rain, Coronavirus? Not bothered. Roll up sleeves, carry on.** Oh, I can't sign with this facemask dangling off one ear. It's swinging around my face like a stripper's bra.

As Saf describes the action, she takes off her cochlear implant, puts it down carefully and takes off the mask. She puts her cochlear implant back on.

Cochlear implant off first, then mask. In that order. Then implant back on.

Let me give you the tour.
She films the caravan on her iPhone, as if on a video call. We see the caravan through the phone's camera.
So here we have the tiny kitchen with the curtains and the original 1970s avocado green and wooden fittings – so cool! And here is the living room at the end of the caravan with tartan banquettes, and a little TV. And this sewing mannequin, taking up space in the middle of the room – that's Steph's best mate. She does her sewing in here. She said she'd clear it out, but I said no, no, leave it in here, we're only staying one night.
Saf suddenly turns the camera to close-up her face.
Famous last words!
Sadness passes over Saf's face for a short moment. Then she brightens.
They decided to increase the Covid restrictions back home, so Steph and Rich said stay here a bit longer. Rich was quite insistent... So I looked at Del and he looked at me, and we were like, yeah, why not? We've got everything we need really, in their front drive in the caravan. The shower's better than our one at home. So we said alright, just for a week – or ten! We don't want to overstay our welcome! But seriously, it's not like we've got to go to work is it. So why the hell not?

We F. U. R. L. O. U. G. H. Work stop temporary. Relax.

Just been to the pub, no less! First time in months. It was alright. The rules are everywhere though aren't they. Makes things awkward.

I said 'Let's walk to the pub, so I can do my steps', but Rich said 'No, it'll rain later.'
So, we had to go in his car.

Mask face, car, get in back seat, next to Steph, sit, press button, open window, fresh air. Normal.

But when I opened my window, for ventilation, Steph raised her eyebrows, and her eyes glinted with mockery, her unmasked mouth twitched in a pitying smile. Rich frowned at me in his rear view mirror and pressed a button to shut my window. He peered back at me. They're both giving me the look that says, 'You're wearing a facemask in a car with us?!' There's a disappointed air – like I've brought orange juice to a party instead of a bag of weed or MDMA. And I'm thinking like, trust me, if I'm bringing the virus to this party, you won't get high on my supply anyway. You will get sick and maybe die.

And I just want to make it clear, about the mask thing, that Rich and Steph are hearing, not deaf, so they don't need to lipread me. So me wearing a mask does not harm them in any way. And they don't like wearing masks much, so I have no problems lipreading them. They sometimes talk a bit too loud, and fingerspell, because they knew me before my implant. I didn't know they were shouting, back then, but I must have noticed their straining faces. I don't say anything, I just turn the volume down a bit.
(She briefly indicates at her processor behind her ear)
Steph and Rich will adapt to my new normal eventually.

Del isn't looking at me as he's sat in front of me. I'm the only person wearing a mask though, and I feel like I've – I've – you know when there's an atmosphere and you're made to feel... like a total dickhead.

Saf begins to hunch her shoulders. Her movements and gait more nervous, less confident.

I know we've just come out of lockdown but I'm not breaking any laws am I? I'm not hurting anyone. I'm not doing anything wrong. We're not out of the woods.
(Beat)
We're in a car.

Saf looks unsure we believe her, and is unsure of herself.

I look at Steph. Her hand makes a cup shape, facing my face. She pats my chin twice with cupped hand.

Saf looks at us as if waiting for a response. Tutting, she demonstrates the hand cupping on the mannequin's face to reinforce the outrage. Clenches her hands anxiously. Withdraws into herself. Quiet voice.

I said... 'You shouldn't touch my mask'. She said, 'Heh heh heh'.

I mean, what do you say? What do you say to that? In the middle of a pandemic! I should have just got out and walked and done my steps and breathed my own air.

We got to the pub garden and things were like...

Normal.

Standard.
Garden, nice. Sat. Pint. Pitter patter. Look up. Rain in eye. Go inside pub. Food served. Mask off slowly. Grin and bear it. Eat lunch. Normal... Keep bubbling anger to myself. Push it down. Carry on.

I said no to a second drink. Said I wanted to walk home and read instead. They said, 'It's going to rain again.' I borrowed the pub umbrella. Del said, 'Do you want me to come?' I said, 'No, you stay, I'm fine, I want to finish my book.'

Saf automatically picks up her phone, clicks on it, looks, then stops herself and puts it down. She picks up a book. She notices someone outside and holds up her book to show them.

Book. (*Nods, smiles*) **Thumbs up!**

Finding her resilience, Saf brightens.

I don't want to make a big deal of it. I'm just saying… it was just a bit of a weird thing to do, you know. I mean I don't want to be judgey. Steph didn't mean to upset me. It was just – an impulse. Everything is so strange and different, and we're all muddling along and making it all up as we go along these days, aren't we.

She picks up a book and settles down to read.

PART 2

A day later. Caravan. Dusk, a light turns on. Saf sits down with a cup of cocoa, in her pyjamas. She looks out of the window, pensive.

SAF

Getting darker earlier. I'll close the curtains in case they see I've already got into my pyjamas.

Saf closes the curtains.

Del's still in there helping to wash up. Things got a bit out of hand. We had a barbecue and Rich… he… he got on my nerves a bit tonight. I don't know why. I mean it was a nice barbecue. I feel bad because I snapped at him when he suggested we play Scrabble. I said, no, I've had enough. Del said, 'Are you alright?'

And I said, 'Yes – no, I'm just tired' and I came back here. I feel a bit embarrassed for snapping after such a lovely barbecue.

BBQ. Enjoying. Sat outside, four around a picnic table. Laughing with R.I.C.H. But awful, his fingers poke my belly. Me, froze, shock.

Saf looks at us confused. She jabs the mannequin's lower abdomen.

Is that weird? Or… Rich jabbed me. I don't know why, maybe because I had a second helping of coleslaw.
There was a lot going on and I just looked at him.

Saf hunches over her phone. She googles on phone. We see her searches, her deletions, her mistypes. She speaks what she types, apart from the typos.

Man… poked (*tuts*)… my… belly… what mean?
MAN PK… (*Deletes 'K'*) POKED MY BELLY. WHAT MEAN

What to do if someone pokes your ab… domen…
WHAT TO DO IF SOOMEONE POKES YOUR AV… ABDOMEN.

Is poking tummy wrong?
IS POKING TUMMY WRONG

Stomach touching pervert.
STOMACH TOUCHING PREVERT

She scrolls, reads, hunches, frowns. Distracted by her phone, she forgets we're there.

PART 3

The next day. Saf looks out of the caravan. She shuts the curtain. There is a white beribboned cake box on the table, unopened.

46

SAF

Can't beat a fresh white cake box with ribbons. Watch me unbox this beauty.
She opens the box and photographs it as she talks.
We walked into the village. It's nice to do normal things, isn't it. They feel more special now.
Steph said, 'Look at this shop,' because the cake display was gorgeous. I took one look, masked up and went in and bought one, because it had been a while, you know. Then when I came out, Rich grabbed me from behind saying, 'Mmm, cake!'. He squeezed my tum. He put his hands on my tum and moved his hand twice. Like this:

She demonstrates on the mannequin.

I jumped away, I stepped back, blurting 'DISTANCE' and 'TWO METRES' and I looked at Steph. Steph looked at me. Through me. And because I'd said 'distance', she looked away and slightly rolled her eyes as well. But it wasn't about that. It was about what he did to my tummy. I know it's just my tummy and it's not like grabbing your tit or worse but you know, it's like grading shit. You can't do it. You can't grade <u>shit</u>.

I walked away, trying to catch up with Del. He was on the phone to someone. He'd not seen what happened. If he'd been there what would have happened. If someone grabs your woman, right in front of you, what happens then?

I'm trying to think if I'd done anything to ask for this. Am I being silly? Is it even a grope if it's a weird area and not the obvious area? I mean, stomach, odd choice. Wrong but odd. But I felt terrible. It made me feel – **disgusted**.

Del was on his phone so I didn't mention anything and it was a busy day after that so… And I started thinking, that because I didn't say anything to Rich at their barbecue about him poking me, maybe I've sort of given Rich permission to do more things. To put both his hands onto my stomach and pull me into his groin. He does it like it's all a bit of normal, harmless everyday fun. It's an escalation of this sort of – fun that he does. But I don't know anyone else who does this to me.

The caravan toilet flushes a few times.

I've just told Del that Rich put his hands on my tummy. I didn't go into too much detail because there's no point us both being upset, and I feel –

Ashamed.

But I said I'm going to say something to Rich about it, right away, if he does it again because he probably doesn't know he's doing anything wrong. Because even though it might be nothing, if I don't stop it, it might happen again.

Del agree. Supports me. Hug.
Saf relinquishes the self hug, as if creeped out by her own hug. As if all hugging is tainted and troubling now.

You have to say something in the second after it's happened. Otherwise it's too difficult. But it's hard to say something. I don't know why it's so hard but it is. I don't want Steph to think I've encouraged him or that I'm imagining that he's flirting with me. And anyway, I don't, I mean I don't know what to think. I don't want to think about what's in his head at all. Because it's just weird and unnecessary. I don't want a row. I just want it to stop. You just want to be able to relax without worrying about being grabbed or poked. That's normal isn't it?

I told Del there was nothing he could do about it. It had to come from me, the moment it happened. If it happened when Del wasn't looking, I'd miss the chance to say something. Del agreed with me. Rich must just not realise he's making me feel uncomfortable. He said that sounded sensible and that he totally supported and believed me.

And I'm so relieved. I love him so much.

And being relieved also makes me re-angry. Because of this nonsense, I've suddenly been put in the position of the possibility of my partner not believing me about being groped. What would have happened if he hadn't believed me? The bottom would have fallen out of my world. I'm not exaggerating. Can you imagine how alone I'd feel if he didn't believe me? I could lose everything because of this pathetic... person.
I'd have to start my life over again. And it's all invisible. What he's doing. No one sees it or feels it but me. It's just between me and him. **Disgusting.**

Hunching. Head dipping, staring into the middle distance. She holds her stomach. Relaxes her hold. It's not her own. A noise outside, laughter of two men and a woman. She looks out the window. She tries to smile.

PART 4
Saf enters the caravan.

SAF
They're playing cards in the back garden.

I made sure I lost. I dropped out early so I could like, disappear. Before he did anything to me.

I can't do it. I can't act normal. Even though Del's there.

I feel like a weirdo. My eyes are darting, I'm tense, I'm clenching my jaw. I can't focus on the usual jokey banter. I'm not taking it in. Rich was talking and I wasn't looking at him because I can't and he said, 'Is it working, have you got it in?'

Saf points at the side of her head, in the style of Rich.

I can't focus on joining in because I have to watch myself, and him. My whole focus is on Rich, anticipating, watching out for his next move so I can be ready for it, ready to move out of the way and say 'No'. I'm ready to fight. Or at least to say, 'No, don't'. I'm on high alert the whole time. Ready to get up and say, 'You touched my knee there, please don't.' Or, 'You stroked my waist, that's not okay.'

Saf stares out, exhausted from anxiety.

PART 5

Crouching down on the floor of the caravan out of view of the window, knees against her chest, Saf hunches over her phone. She reads out what she types, at the same time as typing with her thumbs, mumbling the words. The keys beep as she types.

SAF

Is pat…ting…bum…groping?
IS PATTING BUM GROPING
What – to – do – say – if – some – one – pats – your – bum?
WHAT TO DO IF SOMEONE PATES… PATS YOUR BUM

Saf reads then puts her phone down, sits her bum down on the floor of caravan, and spreads her legs out in front of her, despondent.

There's been a bit of a development, so I'm sitting on the floor because I want to close the curtains but I can't because it's still morning and I don't want to be a drama queen about it.

Del's chopping wood. He didn't see it happen. It always

happens when he's not there.

I said, 'No' to Rich. I said it very firm like that. 'No. Don't pat my bum.'
Maybe I should have said it less bluntly. I don't know. I didn't know what else to say. I can't google in advance can I, because I don't know what he's going to do next.

Last night Del said he reckoned I should 'use humour', but I didn't have time to think of a jokey way of dressing it up. Because I felt frightened. I felt frightened of having to say no to a man whilst I'm making a cup of tea in a kitchen. Being groped making a cup of tea. Why is that even necessary?

And I don't blame me for worrying, because what happened next blew my mind.

Saf is uncomfortable and agitated and she sits on the seating. She punches a cushion. She calms by breathing deeply and demonstrates the movements of people in the anecdote using salt, pepper and some crossword and word search puzzle books.

In the morning Rich squeezed past me in the kitchen in the main house. He didn't have to, there was enough space. Patted me down as he passed. Like this.

Saf shows us on the mannequin. One, two, three. Three light pats, from points at bra strap mid back, to lower back to bum.

He patted his hands down my back and reached my bottom to pat it, and I was ready, like a coiled spring, and I said: 'No, don't pat my bum'…

He won't look at me. Stares at the ground, like he's a small boy. Right away Steph bares her teeth, and says,
(mimics patronising voice)
'Saf darling, he is just being fond of you.'

What?

Fond…

Fondle more like.

'He does that to the kid next door as well because he's just fond of him, that's all.'

Kid next door, wheelchair have. Use wheelchair.

I could barely speak I was so shocked and this all felt too real, and I tried to say he shouldn't poke my abdomen.

It's not gone how I thought it would at all.

I've fucked it now. And Del wasn't in the room at the time. So I'm going to have to wait for a chance to be alone with him and explain what's gone on.

I thought when I said it, Steph would say, 'Oh Rich, what are you like, sorry Saf, he's clumsy'. Acknowledge it, and laugh it off, we'd all be happy with that, and move on. But she got defensive. Steph doing that made it 100 times worse. Made me realise something was clearly very unclear. Very messed up. Very not nice. Very wrong.

Phone WhatsApp chimes. Saf reads the text.

She's asked me to apologise to Rich because I've upset him.

PART 6

It's dark outside. Saf is scrolling her phone. She is crumpled, hunching shoulders, head dipped, low energy.

SAF

It's been the longest day. I've been waiting for the sun to go down so we can go to bed. I didn't reply to her message. I went for a walk with Del and he agreed I had nothing to apologise for. But what is the right thing to do? How can you stop this happening and stay friends?

Googles and reads bits of what she types in monotone.
What – to – do – when – a man – friend…

WHAT TO DO WHEN A MAN FRIEND TOUCHES YOU WITHOUT PERMISSION

Is lower back groping.
IS LOWER BACK GROPING

Is bra strap…
IS BRA STRAP GROPING

How to stop a man groping you
HOW TO STOP A MAN GROPING YOU

HOW TO STOP A MAN TOUCHING YOUR BUM

Is groping illegal.
IS GROPING ILLEGAL?

Google has started advertising weird old man products to me. Horrible looking shoes.

She texts a friends WhatsApp group.
HEY WHAT DO YOU DO WHEN A MALE FRIEND STARTS GETTING TOO HANDSY?

We see the texts superimposed onscreen (as graphics not as part of the subtitles) as she says them.
And they're all like – Vomit emoji,
Are you okay hun?
ARE YOU OKAY HUN?? XXX
Amara is typing now… she's still typing (!): Not cool. Tell him to back off.

NOT COOL. TELL HIM TO BACK OFF.
Saf types fast.
I – did.
I DID!!!!!!
Saf waits for a reply.
Say 'OW' v loud he does it again.

Saf sighs, frustrated and puts her phone to the side.

I want to go home.

PART 7

Saf enters, energised but still hunched. Sits on the edge of a seat. Her phone is charging. She unplugs it and scrolls hungrily, reunited.

SAF

I left my phone charging to stop myself googling the shit out of perverts.

Went for another long walk with Del. Tried not to talk about Rich and Steph. Started making a plan for going home. Leaving politely.

We hadn't been back a minute when Rich grabbed my wrist as I walked past, to ask me if I wanted a coffee. He doesn't need to do that to get my attention. He just needs to say my name. I've told him before. I don't mind people patting my shoulder but that's the one area he hasn't gone for. The one area you're allowed to touch, the one area I'd said is okay: Nah. Not interested.

He grabs my wrist and I go –

She demonstrates with her own hands and wrists.

I yanked my arm away, gently, lifting my arm out and up onto the air with a twist and then down, and she saw this, Steph saw this and nothing was said as usual as per the usual so whatever and I thought, 'hmmm'.

That kind of worked. That worked.

I said no to the coffee so here we are. 'How to stop someone grabbing your wrist'.

HOW TO STOP SOMEONE GRABBING YOUR WRIST.
Oh my –
Saf looks at her phone. She presses play on a video and watches it.

YOUTUBE SELF DEFENCE TUTOR

Hi, and welcome to my self defence demonstration. Today we're going to look at how to stop someone when they grab your wrist.

SAF

Self defence YouTube! Of course. Because Rich is a mate and it's all been happening like in a social domestic situation, I never thought of that – self defence. Not even the blogs about groping at work tell you to use self defence. None of the newspaper articles or anything give you that suggestion. Nobody tells us anything!

Sitting up straight, Saf changes her implant processor setting behind her ear, watches the video (we can't hear it anymore) stands and tries out the self defence move on herself, slowly, move by move.

Swing your hand up into the inside – and straight down to break the grip. Swing up, inside, down. Oh, I can't do it on myself. I'll get Del to do it. Hold on.

Saf, excited, leaves the caravan, banging the door shut.

PART 8
Saf stands transformed, straight backed, calmer, confident in herself.

SAF

Holding your wrist, however gently, is about control and it is an attack.

She demonstrates some moves on the mannequin.

To twist your arm out of an arm grab. To smack an arm out of the way of your lower back. To overpower someone who puts their arm around you.

It works! It actually works!

Saf brims with excitement, as if she wants to convert the world to the joy of self defence.

What no one tells you, is that a basic knowledge of self defence resets you and wards off attack. All forms of attack. And that's the whole moral of this – this – whole rubbish holiday. You don't need to be on high alert if your body is trained to retain the muscle memory of automatic, swift, effective defence and neutralisation of the enemy.
I mean, this is brilliant. I learnt some more moves off YouTube, and Del –

Saf tries to show the moves on the mannequin.

He helped me rehearse the moves in the garden... and I saw a curtain twitch.

And then, we had a barbecue lunch with them, and I didn't get groped, squeezed, grabbed, stroked or poked for the rest of the day. So he must have seen. Result!

But also, I was cheerful. I was on form. I was me. This has changed everything. It's changed me. How I am, how I carry myself! I don't need to be on edge anymore. No more flight or fight mode.

I've googled some martial arts classes and obviously that's going to be hard because everything is shut. But I will learn. I know that it's about being neutral in yourself.
Me being on edge was what he wanted. It's a type of power or control. So what you need is to not be infected by their nonsense, to demand personal space and distance through self defence, to be neutral and not anxious. Not even thinking of him.

He knows that if he invades my space and touches me that he will get dominated by proportionate force. I don't know if he thinks I will hurt him. But it's the act isn't it. I won't go over the top. I will just make it proportionate. A light, firm twist and off. No pain, all the gain. Brilliant.
And that's it. That's how to deflect the sad-arse, bog standard, pervert in your life. I probably won't have to do anything, once I'm trained up, because he won't come near me now.

Saf takes up a martial arts stance and speaks her new mantra.

Reset yourself to neutral; know the moves; carry the muscle memory of those moves. All power to you girl. All power to you.

Alison Campbell
After the Row

After the row, I'll shout,

Don't follow me!
Slam the front door, toss my long scarf

over my shoulder,
so that the orange tassels flick my back.

I won't see you turn away
from the window.

I'll walk down the road,
look back, catch sight of the gate

swinging empty. I'll weave through the traffic,
wave to the blue Fiesta

slowing for me – catch myself pausing
by the zebra crossing, think, should I turn back now?

But I'll join the pavement stream, past plantain and yam
in plastic bowls, and the Big Yellow car-wash.

I'll stop to pick up a Metro – swoop for the last one,
my heavy bag will bump down on my legs.

I'll hitch the strap back on my shoulder,
carry on walking, glance towards the lit entrance

of the deep tube. It's my last chance to turn.
There's a nodding helium balloon,

translucent and red with sparkly stars,
caught by its string on the traffic lights.

It's then that I'll wish you'd come after me –
had seen that I'm full of hot air.

Ksenia Balabina
Circus of Change

A man stands in an arena, with the spotlight shining down on him, illuminating his exaggerated features.
First, you see a wild mop of bushy red hair, then eyes are drawn to the white around the eyes, a bright red nose, and a painted mouth.
An oversized bow around his neck, dressed in a suit covered in colourful dots. He stands there in his gigantic shoes.
He looks out at the audience and they laugh.
He walks towards people, tripping over his shoes. Hysterical laughter fills the air.

On a seemingly empty red chair, he notices something and approaches to see a small figure, still, with painted smile.
She has lopsided plaits, eyelashes off kilter, clothes dirty and torn.
The man reaches out and takes her in his arms.
He still smiles, but there is a sadness in his eyes.

The audience do not notice and continue laughing.

He carries the girl back to the spotlight in the arena, stands there, still smiling.
The audience now are unsure, confused – should they laugh or not?

He speaks loudly to the audience.
'People are quick to judge on appearances.

You think she is ignorant, and has no language of her own?'
The people in the audience look around at each other.
'You think she has no education and doesn't know what to do?
What if she is deaf and can't hear what we are saying? What if
she is scared and can't express herself?'

The audience are frozen in their seats.

The man goes on. 'With this paint on my face, you think I'm the
joker, the clown who makes you laugh, but I am the opposite
of this rag doll.' He raises his hand and wipes it across his face,
smearing his make-up to reveal a deep frown and states,
'I am broken on the inside.'

The light goes out.

David Callin
Coastal Walking for the Hard of Hearing

The wind is a bully, in hearing aids:
making itself
and nothing else heard.
So out they come,
and calm is restored,
the world reduced to a silent film.

Diane Dobson
Walking is an Option

Storm Desmond.
Out on site,
high winds,
horizontal rain.
This coat's not waterproof.
Soaking wet
freezing cold
back twists –
searing pain
barely make it home.

Hospital scans.
Ruptured disc.
Big bottle of morphine –
We trust you with it
5-10ml every four hours
Still in agony
it just takes the edge off.
Flat on back
staring out the window
cloud watching
that one's a horse
that one's a whale
that one's a… cloud.

More bottles of morphine.
Can't stand the stuff.

Night time's the worst
no sleep
watching the spiders
crawl across the ceiling.
Cat jumps on bed
curls up on my chest
gentle rumbling purrs,
I drift away
for half an hour.

Come on you need to eat.
I'm not hungry

I can't do this.
Yes, you can
No, I can't.
Yes, you can.
I can't.

Enticements of mashed potato
a few spoons more each day
veggie sausage and peas.
How about a few tinned peaches?
Toast for breakfast,
crumpets for tea.

Occupational therapist.
Come on get up
Take two or three steps

I can't do this.

Yes, you can.
No, I can't.
Yes, you can.
I can't.

Three more steps,
more each day,
Then pacing Dad's bungalow

Last dose of morphine…
I bin it instead.
On four different painkillers
Side effects of constipation.
Going to the toilet
is a scream
Literally.
Battling withdrawal symptoms
Weeks of sickness and stomach cramps.

I can't do this.
Yes, you can.
No, I can't.
Yes, you can.
I can't.

Step outside Dad's back door
fresh spring air, birds singing.
Short walk down the road
further each day,
make it to the crossroads
then back up the hill to Dad's.

*Try meditation
it'll help with the pain.
Imagine a golden light,
breathe it in
then breathe out the pain*
Ten minutes of shining a light
pain not budging.

I can't do this.
Yes, you can.
No, I can't.
Yes, you can.
I can't.

*You're trying too hard.
Untense, relax
focus on your breathing.
Breathe in one two three four
breathe out one two three four*
Meditating each day
five minutes
six minutes
ten minutes
small moments of stillness.

Back to work on half days.
Can't sit for long,
can't stand for long.

I can't do this.
Yes, you can.
No, I can't.
Yes, you can.
I can't.

Get up.
Go to work
longer days,
then back full-time.

Summer passes
with meditation, stretching exercises
back brace on for site visits.
Then, standing in rivers
water flowing past my fingers
pebbles shifting under my feet.

Autumn descends.
Long walks along the lake shore
watching ripples on the surface
diffuse reflections of golden yellows and browns.

The first sprinkling of snow on the fell tops
frost coating bare branches.
Then bitter cold mornings
with crisp clear blue skies.

Is life back to normal?
No, the pain is still there,
but – I can do this.

Clare-Louise English
A Word of Warning

We're going on an adventure, just you and I
we're going to sit out under the night sky
we'll make toasts to each other, and drink till we weep
but a word of warning, don't eat the sheep.

We're off to the country, my four-legged friend
we're off to follow footpaths that meander and bend
we'll dream of success and catch up on sleep
but please god, just – don't eat the sheep.

We're going to a shepherd's hut found on Airbnb
we're going to explore my pointy-nosed pedigree
we'll paddle in streams that don't run too deep
but whatever happens, don't eat the sheep.

We're going to cook outside on a barbecue
we're going to sit for hours and relish the view
we'll lie back and listen to the birds going tweet
but I'm asking you nicely, don't eat the sheep.

We're going on an adventure just you and I
we'll inhale freedom and breathe out a sigh
we'll know true calmness as into our bones it seeps
but please, please, I beg of you, please, don't eat the sheep.

Jay Caldwell
Wagging the Dog

My mind pulls my body up, pushes me out the
door on one end of an extendable lead. Watch
her tail, it says, see how happy she is, it says.
And it's not wrong. So I stumble down the
street, gasping as feet and knees jar with each
step, and gradually my gaze lifts from the
metronomic blur of her tail to her perked ears,
and beyond to white valerian shooting from the
bottom of a red wall, the dazzling light-green
leaf sprigs of privet, the self-seeded hollies
holding out their papier-mâché pink buds for
shy approval, and the cherry-pop blossom
waving over the hedge. And I think, ok mind,
you're not wrong, my tail is wagging.

Samantha Baines
Quiet Twosome

She can't speak and I can't hear and that suits us very well,
we are a quiet twosome.

A twitch of her head lets me know she's angry,
she raises her nose to ask 'what's for dinner?'
and if she's very frustrated she will pee on my bed
(once she even peed on my ex).

Queen Victoria is a cat,
she flicks her litter around the room,
she claws at my most expensive furniture,
she sniffs at my hair when it needs a wash.

She doesn't meow much,
she knows there's not much point,
without my hearing aid I miss her little mews,
but she has learnt how to deal with me.

In the morning she will paw my face to show she's ready to start the day.
If she's lying nearby and wants to be stroked she will stretch out one paw and poke me.
I can't always tell if she's purring,
so I put my cheek to her stomach, and she lets me.

She runs to the door when the postman comes,
alerting me he's there before he rings the bell.
She loves actual tuna but not tuna in cat food,
she likes classical music and hates gun fights on TV,
and she will absolutely under no circumstances wear a collar.

Mostly we sit in silence as she warms my feet
and I sip my tea.
She will paw at my wool as I create,
bite at my toes through the blanket if I wiggle them
but most of all she accepts the quiet.

Not two, perhaps we are three. The quiet, my cat and me.

Rodney Wood
de Belder Guido
The inventor of Magical Abstract Realist Romanticism, an artistic style of which he was the sole practitioner. He meticulously documented the movement in a 150-page manifesto which has sadly been lost.

He was tired of dancing round people
to make sure they were on the right side
or walking with his head at right angles,
crashing into lampposts, ladders, stepping
into puddles or him saying
                              I'm sorry,
could you say that again?
                              For his art
he gave up the sound of everything:
the sea wearing itself out against the beach,
someone saying, *I love you,* wind waiting
in the trees, craters the rain makes almost
every day here, people talking with voices
that almost make sense, stupid jokes, the cat
meowing to be let in, the kettle boiling
but these are small things that cry out for more.

Some days were depressing and didn't make
sense but other days were beautiful.
He hid away and the silence meant
he could work in a paradise.

Lisa Kelly
A Map Towards Fluency

I. Bedrock
I map a--to my left thumb

Alex maps a-------------------------------------to his right thumb

e--to my left forefinger

poor Alex, the teacher can't map sinistral--------------to dextral
thesaurus maps sinistral----------------------------------to sinister
a hammer mapped a red line-------------to his drummer's hand

i---to my left middle finger
(Sophie maps i----------------------------------to her *swear finger*)

o---------------------------------------to the gold of my ring finger
u---to my left pinkie

map a twist of fist in the gut-------------------------------to hate
a raised pinkie thrust forward---------------------------------to bad
an open palm on the heart------------------------------------to like
finger men meet---to greet

hands beckon a welcome-------------------------------at waist level
the weight of weather---------------at the altitude of cheekbones

Helena, who can't remember the palm-to-palm swish of her capital *H*
marks each digit with a marker pen-------------------------------*a*
---*e*
---*i*
---*o*
---*u*

(is this cheating?)

II. Deposition of Sediment
Words are shifting animals
                        a fish is a handshimmer
a cat is claws, preening whiskers
                        a bird, a forefinger beaking a thumb

Colours clothe the body in a flash of flesh
Red *brushes* lips   Blue *strokes* veins on wrist
Green *grazes* forearm   Black *knuckles* cheek
Pink *taps* nose   White   *flares*   fingers

What has happened to Alex?
        Helena has changed her shift, and is here
Late from an audition, Sophie circles sorry at the centre of her chest, her cheeks
a tapped nose

We bring our colours and animals with us
                Helena, a forefinger beaking thumb,
                settles on the edge of her chair
                Alex, an absent handshimmer

III. Outcrop

                    Jean
               our teacher
            is a landmark
         All eyes look to her
      What can you see out of your
   peripheral vision? Furrows forming
and reforming on ever-more familiar faces
Gestures formed and reformed by ever-more
familiar hands: rings, scars, tattoos. We keep our
distance. Eyes cannot whisper. Air, larynx, tongue:
all fingers and thumbs. As a child, Jean was forced to
sit on her hands. *Don't point! Don't touch!* Now her hands
guide us towards an alternative view. She signs, we are touched

IV. Precious Minerals

                                Context is everything

We are unearthing

                                the philosopher's stone

Base metal can be turned into   a fist
                                    on a fist
                                    flexing into splayed fingers

Bank is   a fist with thumb cocked, stamping the palm
Aid is   a fist with thumb up, proffered on the palm
How old?   fingers dance on the nose
How much? fingers dance on the chin
Alex is in   a heavy metal band

On a world tour without him, it is laughing all the way to
        the fist with thumb cocked, stamping the palm

Helena's fingers dance on her chin

On a world tour without him, it cannot offer
                a fist with thumb up, proffered on the palm

Alex says he is feeling his age

Sophie's fingers dance on her nose

V. Erosion
I imagine our hands chopped off as Philomela had her tongue cut out
What would there be to say? How would we say it?
Not able to weave our stories into a tapestry
Alex unable to drum his rhythm. Sophie
unable to sign her song. Helena
unable to recall her felt-tipped
fingers. Alex laughs, which
is how it should be
We are going our
separate ways
towards fluency
and erosion
The future
a hand thrust
forward
the past
a wave
over the
shoulder

Elizabeth A Ward
Loops

I cast a line of woollen loops
onto a needle, ready to begin:
like the loops of a spring
holding and spreading weight
or feet ready to jeté from the ground.

The casting on is only a beginning,
as I hook the second needle through
ravelling lines of neat garter stitch:
a chorus row of interlocking limbs
waiting in the wings of a mise en scène.

I feel the click each time a loop
slides from one needle to the next,
a rhythmic note speeding up:
a heartbeat, a dance, a sidestep –
wide untraversed space between us.

The casting off, a neat two rounds,
nestled together for a short moment:
as I slide one over another, back and
forth, leapfrog, but bound together,
the selvedge of a chain of lives.

Colly Metcalfe
Coffee Shop

The lunchtime queue in the coffee shop is long.
A hundred (well, ten) chatty, sweaty customers in front of
me, waiting to be served; feet moving – shuffling – tapping
impatiently...
I watch their conversations, surreptitiously; sliding my gaze
away, swiftly and
expertly...
never quite getting caught
eavesdropping.

I know their secrets.
I see their stories on their lips, their boasts and their fibs,
I see them talking.
I know who's shagging who,
I know who's nicking off and who hates the boss.

I see all of their animated water-cooler politics and...
the queue moves along.

Baristas' arms are flying, grains of coffee spilling.
The WHOOSHing, SHOOSH of the hot water spout
spitting out the clean steam and...
the queue moves along.

Eight people in front of me.
I know my order; rehearsed and ready. No dithering and time
wasting;

no umming and erming, no debating, procrastinating –
ONE LARGE SKINNY HOT CHOCOLATE TO GO,
PLEASE
(Smiley face ☺)

Three people are in front of me.
My heart starts to beat
faster....
my eyes sweep the space;
I search for the benevolent face of an understanding barista
as they perform their arm choreography behind the counter.

Latte, flat white, Americano-to-go... 'Any hot food today?'
I see her say...

IT'S HER!
She has a kind face and her words are clear to see
on shiny pink lips,
tattoos on her wrists and her hair in braids.

Heart slows its pace.
Words paused on tip-of-tongue ready. Pink lips looks up, eye contact, smiles
I breathe in and...
SHE LEAVES!
She takes her smile and her kind eyes, she moves away and I see her say '...a quick break...'

A surly faced girl steps into her place to take my order.
– I waver.

I see her say something – is she talking to me? There are still two people in front –
have they been served?
Have they ordered??
Do I speak now??
Is it me now???
HAVE THEY PAID??
She hasn't looked up yet; hasn't found my gaze and…
the queue moves along.

Surly girl's lips move again and I wait, my eyes scanning the space for clues. Who's next?
I can't tell… I freeze. Shuffling feet and…
the queue moves along.

I lock eyes with surly girl and I half smile, half breathe in and she moves her lips to
THE GUY BEHIND ME
her silent words shout – 'can I take your order, sir?' Her eyes meet again with mine; she smirks.
I feel… small – yet glaringly big and conspicuous with my lack of hot chocolate and… the queue moves along.

Oh… DILEMMA.
I gather my dignity, regroup my courage, find my voice, take back my choice and I halt the shuffling feet behind me

I hold up my hand 'Excuse me!'
(Is my voice too harsh? Too soft?? It's hard to gauge when it's loud around.)

The Whole Queue Stops Moving. Irritated eyes stab behind; queue-mates questioning the delay.
I can't hear them, but I know they're tutting. Muttering, mumbling, accusing.
Surly girl's eyes square up to meet mine in a
challenge of
threatening customer service

I say – 'Sorry (not sorry), but I haven't ordered, and you've served the man behind…'
Surly eyes stay locked on mine, surly girl she replies:
'So, I asked you, like, THREE TIMES (rolls eyes) for your order and you, like, ignored me,
so… blur, blur, blur…'
She turns her face away and her words chase her gaze. No clear shapes for me to read,
just people – looking at me. 'Well, can I order now please? I didn't see you speak to me,
I can't hear your words and
I didn't know it was my turn;
I couldn't see you behind the haze of customers and sunshine…'
I'm blushing; flushing, flummoxed and flustered. My words tumble, jumbled; explaining my CAN'T.

Surly girl… sighs
out of the corner of my eye
I spy
shiny pink lips, tattoos on her wrists and her hair in braids…

walking towards me. She catches my eye and as she smiles, she lifts her dancing barista arms and… SIGNS
Hello; what would you like?
I grin. I breathe in and…
Surly girl looks sheepish; fellow queue-mates look guilty, and I feel my power return.
I sign:
ONE LARGE SKINNY HOT CHOCOLATE TO GO, PLEASE
(Smiley face ☺)

Alison Campbell
Paper bags always meant one thing

Chocolate is only permitted when the Aunt
brings bags of broken bits from her factory job
at Lindt, shared between eight.

The village matrons never keep their counsel.
Guzzling again? You should be helping
your father on the farm!

The sisters would block their ears . When they could take
no more, the spruce woods gave sanctuary –
edelweiss, martagon lilies and shade.

Without words, they'd strip, shout and scream
around bundles of boots, in wide whirling circles,
within the zoetrope of dark trees.

They'd return in a line, hems askew,
covered in pine needles, to potato-digging,
weeding and hoeing – dreaming of Aunt's packages.

Years later, they'd leave – away from the call of the farm.
On rare visits back, they nibble *Kägi fret*,
on lakeside picnics. Amber-roofed farms

fleck the far mountains. Village voices echo
but they don't live there now – have no stake.
Instead, they smile and talk fondly of Lindt.

Kägi fret – chocolate covered waffles

Julie Boden
Fish and a Blue-Arsed Fly

I used to be a blue-arsed fly;
toured Cork, Kolkata, Dublin, Rome,
Valencia, Ghent, Milan, Mumbai
but these days I must stay at home.

Toured Cork, Kolkata, Dublin, Rome,
invited to read poetry,
but these days I must stay at home.
Inside these walls I'm all at sea.

Invited to read poetry
before this illness grew within.
Inside these walls I'm all at sea,
now, fish – without gill, tail or fin.

Before this illness grew within
I used to travel everywhere.
Now, fish – without gill, tail or fin
I'm lost in water; lost in air.

I used to travel everywhere
Valencia, Ghent, Milan, Mumbai.
I'm lost in water; lost in air.
I used to be a blue-arsed fly.

Marilyn Longstaff
Sea Pool

Tongue, tonsils, coated
with foul white thrush

her throat strains
against the outgoing tide.

On the surface,
all seems calm, flattened

by cold wet breath of fog.

But something nameless
is lurking in her depths.

These are not her seasons
not her colours.

She is out of her time
must let go.

Drift.

Lynn Buckle
Ailbhe's Tale

Few women are employed in the tanning, currying, and dressing of leather. Ailbhe Sarah Kelly is one of them.
Not much survives the wharf, where tannins stain river water, leak through marsh, seep into feeders. The tannery harnesses ample water supplies, without too much loss of product.

In addition to creating potentially toxic wastewater, some tanneries produce large amounts of solid waste that contain chromium, including hide scraps, skins, and excess fats. The environmental impact statement recorded exceptional levels of contaminants in effluent samples.

TPA Fashions uses vegetable-tanned leather, rather than chrome-based products.

'You do realise that hides are from cows?'

Offal is the only intended loss. Oft flung across to the island which floats between river and bog. A place too wet for anything other than the dumping of rotten carcasses. The river being measured by the distance women can effectively fling dead, slippery things. The place at which the river bends is the widest. It is simple mathematics not to stand there but adjacent to the wooden bridge where the river is at its narrowest. However, flinging is banned at this point due to frequent near misses which result in an offal back-up. That changes the course of the water.

Eels gather to feed upon the spillage. Some say it is the fault of Ailbhe Sarah Kelly.

Some say I was born a runt, that I would never amount to much of a thrower.

'She hasn't the heft to fling a carcass clear of six yards, nine inches, and three eighths (depending on rain). Any decent flinger could clear that gap with a large heifer.'

'Unless they were lazy with the innards.'

'She was told to keep her legs on the riverbank, to get out of the water.'

'She is slow to listen.'

'She must be feeding the eels.'

Gangers pooled around her, drawn to weaklings like eels to blood.

Eventually, we post her on the far side of the river. It is her job to haul the flung meat to the centre of the boggy island patch. The resulting pile of entrails, boiled bones, and bloated stomachs becomes a target practise for some. The pile undulates with its own gasses, legs waving involuntarily with each exhalation of methane and rancid fluid.

We find that peat is powerfully acidic and that it has analogous properties with respect to the tanning of leathers, quoad the preservation of dead bodies.

A stranger could easily mistake them, everyone says, for humans. Polite society avoids the wooden bridge with its indecorous views and stench, avoids the village. It is Ailbhe Sarah Kelly's fault, for being a deaf one.

I watch to listen, and still they come.

The independent Standing Scientific Committee on Eels sets targets of quantities to be transported annually.

I left, eventually, conveyed on waters flowing eastwards.

The Bog of Allen is raised, at its highest elevation, about two hundred and seventy feet above the Liffey at low water in Dublin.

'All downstream from here then.'

There are prolific numbers of eel fish awaiting transportation to foreign markets, while the export market in tanned hides is decreasing.

'Impregnated, she was, by the eels,' they said, 'her fault for standing in the water.'

But you, with your curse, are destined to wander alone.

She flowed with the Liffey into Dublin, where all rivers meet, her growing belly swelling. The eels chased her still.

A map of Dublin waterways named after women. Researched and drawn by a bookbinder living on the quays.

She found the many streams, to be guided around the city using female lines, the spaces in between, the buried rivers and culverts where she birthed and left her baby swimming, a translucent elver of a thing. Left to suck at inlets.

Adverse reproductive outcomes associated with maternal exposure to leatherwork include; an increased risk of prenatal death, spontaneous preterm delivery, low birth weight, cleft palate, [and hearing loss] (Garcia and Fletcher, 1998).

She stood under dock walls, to keep the water in her feet, and dipped them into ports. She submerged herself in harbours, swam around piers, until she knew the water-swell and felt the salty tide pull her out and in.

She was forever treading, testing, reading brine until one perfect night, when waves flattened out, she swam into the Irish Sea and did not come back. Her strokes lifted phosphorescence from the surface and *tine shionaigh* shone all about. Like will-o'-the-wisps of dancing light over bog water, they flashed of home. So she kept on swimming, with seaweed in her locks. She swam alongside sailors, past and present, who demanded her presence. They wrapped about her legs and pulled down towards dark fathoms, where all things drift. Where they mixed with elvers of glass and slipped between her toes. She raced against such tidal currents, among streams of migrating fish. It was no distance at all for the eels, who had come 3,700 miles, from Sargasso seas, to follow instincts. And she continued on with her breaststrokes.

The European Court of Justice prohibits Ireland from suing the UK before the Tribunal of the Law of the Sea on the grounds that it is polluting the Irish Sea with nuclear waste.

Milling the waves, her arms rotated as blades through wind, and she imagined great farms harnessing wild powers. For rest she lay on her back, otter-like, and cracked shells with hardened teeth.

If only I consumed less energy, I would not be in this predicament.

She swam for so long that she swallowed salted, jellied eels and heard their souls a-calling. She could not stop listening, for laments are easily felt through the skin. There were so many choruses near rocky outcrops that she swam about them, taunting the persistent eels. They chased her into the English Channel, which she traversed so quickly, and into Northern waters. The accent of water may have changed, but its flavour remained the same. Eventually she turned into Yarmouth's Yare, a maiden voyager with eels in her hair.

Eels are one of the most demanding species of saltwater fish. Which would be nice, if transporting eels were an end in itself. But the object is surely to increase the eel population, and I note that the minister had nothing to say on that subject. Nor did he tell what the stock of eels was. So, we have no idea whether all this activity is achieving anything, and responsibility is diffused amongst the members of a Standing Scientific Committee on Eels, none of whom seem to have any stake in the matter.

Even the Norfolk Broads were infested with fresh and mature species. They snaked through reeds, and hugged silt after winding there from chalky reefs. Always stalking.

She swam the River Wensum, and all its connecting waters, under dulling suns and heaving airs. She out-swam the predators who cat-called and whistled from the banks. She heard them when she heard them not, as she dredged the riverbeds of their scum, unblocked their ditches, flooded fens, unleashed reinforcements against floodwaters, as she swam.

…and you keep a kayak for this purpose in your back garden, for the floods will surely send you elsewhere on eventual tides of climate change. Send you from one tannery to another as rivers, canals, bog waters, rise and you flow to apprentice tanner Saint William of Norwich whose trade came down maternal lines. Learning his sainthood from the gaps in between all of these.

Ensuring water quality in rivers and Broads can help only remaining populations.

Ailbhe Sarah Kelly built her own tannery, on pilings driven into the Wensum, sinking sounds and muffling vibrations. She caused ripples building a business and a quiet life, using vegetable dyes and mineral-free techniques. When questioned about her methods, it was her marital status they meant, her finances, her industry. Her liberty. She turned her head away that she may not see what they said. When pressed, she replied,

'I do not need to pander to you while eels still turn about my ankle. You say I do not hear. You do not hear my fears.'

'I like that idea – remind me to go and do some digging in the river. Where are you getting all this information from? Eels are not men.'

Dr Raymond Pendergrast says there are no elver traps operating on the River Wensum.

Pike and three-spined stickleback, bitterns, stoats, and water voles in habitats preserved. Otters being the gateway animal to public sentimentality, the soft drug of conservation.

She fought acts of Parliament which raised capital for river navigation improvements. They made savage cuts to her re-wilding work as they re-built embankments, re-routed and buried her water.

This greenhouse effect, land is melting away.

They closed off her direct channel to the cathedral, Pull's Ferry, for fear she would taint its holy grounds. They could not close her off. She let the water free again.

A local businesswoman has outraged public decency under common law and has been charged for immersing herself, fully clothed, in marsh waters on the outskirts of the city of Norwich. Following two warnings, she was arrested on foot of a bill issued by local yeomanry, who became alarmed at her continuous presence in the water. When asked if she understood the charges brought against her, the woman declined to comment and kept her head turned to the left. She did not see her sentence being read.

She swam underwater after that, eyes wide open, looking for cleaner waters, and knew her years spent starboard in foreign waters were coming to an end. Flailing, swimming, building, never listening, she was never really held by those tannery's wooden pilings. She yearned for other watery foundations, for warm smells of softened beer smoking over cobbles, for Dublin's channels, wet Midlands pastures, her native bog water for tanning, and for swimming.

Returning to her home-country, 'Mrs' Kelly becomes the canal's first incumbrancer, funding it to the sum of £135,000. Were it not for the diabolical atrocity of 1856, the spinster would still be whoring her mortgage of the Grand Canal.

She financed the canal's construction, beating the eels at their game. Swimming.

...& there is a rare place, where the water and the wind unrefrains.

Josephine Dickinson
Bones Under Their Feet

The forest moves half a mile a year. Can you think of a
single thing which does/ not depend on structures or
concept of language? the distant stars?/

can we perceive them without language? can they exist
without our perception?/ Do you promise not to tell? I'll
tell you if you promise not to tell./

The flock of birds assumed the shape of a bird before
settling./ In the yellow sulphur light a moth swings
moonlike, mobile./

The blackbird, simple blackbird, who has no other name
but a colour,/ trapped between the two walls of barley,
lurches from side to side./

I wanted to lie down there in the wet grass and stay
there all night. A gaggle of/ guards in smart uniforms,
the legendary brutes, giggled as I asked the way./

Don't run out this Christmas. No. It's June. The luxurious
growth spills over the/ bank. Stud the bank, the yellow
flowers, the bits of yellow, the spikes of yellow,/

the hand grabs of yellow. Buildings begin to rear like
paintings. The only reason/ these creatures with
luxurious growth flowing from their heads/

don't get up and run when they see me is that I look like
one of them./ One more stitch over the needle and then
another step./

Red colour, red fuzz fur. She slammed the table with an iron like a wedding cake./ Everything went quiet in the train except that the train was making/

a lot of noise. I'm held together by the milky way. The island city is opening up/ to the desert. Rise above the cooling of the city and its heating He spent a long/

time closing the door quietly. The concrete pillar divides the singer/ from the synthesizer. Tent flaps in the dark. I tread carefully, then/

more boldly, feel moving bones under my feet then, swung/ under their pole, a light flashes. I am bones under their feet./

Again, again the swing of light. Everything grows upward. Blown by the wind/ in the dark what can I do to find your shores?/

What are those white numbers painted on the brown wall: 43, 42, then,/ suddenly, 30, 35 on the weeping iron, 33, 32, 31?/

A clock by the bedside. Gertrude Stein would approve. Above the sea/ of faces one looked down and smiled. Why put lots of bricks on roof ?/

A copy of Theaetetus tucked under his arm, hand sewn pink shirt, dark pressed/ trousers, tufted hair. He learned to read in a classroom with salty floorboards./

I sometimes wondered what it would be like if I went up to one of them, said here/ you are and wrote them a cheque for all my wealth. It's aching, this hand:/

five more minutes and I'll have a rest — not that it's very heavy,/ this paper cola cup. I couldn't find anything else and my hat fell/

off the bridge. I stand as straight as I can, how my mother told me./ I'll assume I'll meet you there unless I hear otherwise... Hallo.../

hallo.../

How long does one have to wait before X walks past? She ran back/ into the Ladies room in black muslin calling 'Babs!'/

I caught him looking at her, thinking no one saw him./ Trees are not fearful of height. How long before a friend happens to pass?/

Joe needs to leave behind him the rhetoric of the boardroom (which/ has more hold over him still than he realises because, in discouraging/

archetypes, the scientific/business world promotes the greediest archetype/ of them all — reality) and allow himself to be seduced by things in themselves — /

a rose is a rose is a rose.

Charlie Swinbourne
DeLorean

A roll of their eyes and my
DeLorean flies me back
Past sixteen houses and seven cars
Two babies and three gaps

Before Hooch and Diamond White
Zinger Tower Burgers and Marlboro Lights
The news of that December morning
And the blackness of forgotten nights

To a real, blue-eyed living boy
Who couldn't say his s's
And had no idea
That he'd mistaken all his guesses

The scaffolding went up bit by bit
With hands of wood and eyes of stone
A smile was etched upon his face
The room was crowded, but the boy alone

The wood started to bend
And the stone began to crack
His eyes opened to see
A strange world staring back

The boy got up and staggered
Tripped and fell and landed
Through dust and rain and snow and fog
His broken bones slowly mended

When he came upon a place
Between the sand and the sea
Between speech and sign, loud and quiet
And the boy began to breathe

My DeLorean reverses
Past twelve thousand eye rolls and smirks
One head butt and nineteen insults
To now
Where I explain again that I just misheard

Ayesha B Gavin
Sense of Direction

Do quiet roads lead within
as you lie upon your bed,
Are there maps that open
the connections in your head?

The compass needle points south,
but the sat nav sends you right.
What happens if you go straight,
follow star, not satellite?

Are you frightened? Are you lonely?
Do you want to feel alive?
Do you care where you are taken
on your psyche's midnight drive?

Can you know where you started from
before memory begins?
Is this just a gentle jaunt
or a race you have to win?

As you travel on your roads
with knowledge to pay the toll
you'll learn the layout of your heart,
the topography of soul.

There are answers, explanations,
is an exit somewhere near?
Believe in maps you made yourself –
nothing to fear, but fear.

Hala Hashem
Where is Syria?

Grew up in London from the age of five
in a strange new country and struggling to settle
it was confusing with the funny looks I got
and having my name mispronounced
not forgetting being constantly questioned
if I lived in a desert, in a tent with camels?
continuously kept me tested.

Oh how often I was asked 'Where is Syria?'
the country of my birthplace and my heritage.
So widely unknown this country was
with distant echoes of 'never heard of it'.
Having to explain where exactly it was
below that well known country of Turkey.
People's eyes then lit up with understanding
I had prayed they passed on this discovery.

Oh Syria was
Where once I spoke and sang Arabic as a child
Where often I heard the beauty of Arabic music
Where often I smelled heavenly Arabic dishes
wafting in the air in my grandma's kitchen
Where often I spent wonderful holidays
with my family and all our relatives
Where often I explored its rich historical ruins
and uncovered its precious jewels.

Oh our hearts broke when the tragic war unfolded
as our little known Syria got splashed on the news.
Amidst worries and prayers for our relatives there
I saw an outpouring of love and sorrow
from strangers all around the globe
for a beautiful country shattered
and for millions of its people scattered.
Because of this it's bitter sweet
that no more do people ask me 'Where is Syria?'
People all over know where Syria is now.

Ayesha B Gavin
In Memory of our Father

Mohammad Azfar 1927-2010

I found a map the other day
of a country that no longer exists.
It shows where our father was born and raised –
before a political shift.

White men came to set up trade
 to promote their own interests
 in cotton, indigo, saltpetre and tea.
The people, as slaves, were next.

Same old story, our father would say –
those in charge divide and conquer.
That classic strategy –
set religions apart, not together.

Neighbours of old bought what was sold
and took up arms for their faith.
Our father would tell of a violent hell
he witnessed before he was eight.

The leaders decreed a solution –
the map would be rendered in two.
One side for the Muslim
the other for the Hindu.

Our family was part of the exodus –
Muslims to the new promised land.
Questioned and curfewed, they fled to the west –
the crescent and star of Pakistan.

Father would sometimes speak of his past
and tell of his life as a child.
Will the peoples of that great country
ever be reconciled?

At times when we asked him his story
he'd gaze at the horizon and say,
'There's peace in these meadows of Glasgow.
You won't know my hardships, I pray.'

Though our father was taken with failing heart,
his knowledge and light will go on
for the map of his journey still hangs on the wall.
And the truth can't be undone.

Janet Hatherley
One or Two Interesting Facts About Dad

My dad fought in both World Wars,
being just old enough

for the First
and just young enough

for the Second.
He had shrapnel in his right ear—

doesn't always hear me when I ask,
What did you do in the wars, Dad?

Janet Hatherley
With My Back to the Wall

I'm thirteen, discover I have hearing loss
in my right ear too. *Did Dad pass it on to me?*

I don't talk much. I listen hard, watch people's lips,
hang back from groups,

tease out voices from background noise.
Why are you sat at the front of the class?

I stare through the window at the water tower
in East Wittering, eight miles, as the crow flies home

across winter fields. Every term my name is called,
all eyes on me as I stand up, walk out.

My footsteps echo off the white corridor walls
to the nurse's room.

I can see her finger on the button,
know when the sound will come, high or low.

The final straw, pulled out of a cookery exam,
I decide enough is enough,

wait for her finger to push the button.
Press, *Yeh…* Press, *Yeh…* I fake the test,

move from the front row to the back of the class.

Sophie Stone
I , Nyx: (A Daughter's Daughter)

i.
'Can you feel me rising?' she said as I lay heavy in bed,
the whisper of dawn through thick curtains.
It's been a long night and still
I fight to wake.

Dormant sounds underground, await my stir.
But,
drunk on starlight gazing
like when we counted satellites passing above
us, lying on rooftops of cars, I
wish to not move just yet

She said 'I'll wait.
I'll give you time.
This is your Epilogue, not mine.
This is your Fermata, your Breve Rest,
so breathe.
Take what you need.
I'll rise when I'm heeded, don't anticipate me, it brings
no music and
therefore
no food.

When I do come, I shall sing.
I shall bring mist after moonshine and you'll see
                antlers
dance on fields of clouds.

I won't stay long.
It's not my time to shine.'

ii.
She drifted North
motivating the seeds beneath her feet.
Buried

but alive—
    reaching
yearning

    for the blinding, burning arch
of light.

'Pour your hibernated, resistant shards, as if arriving home to
your Ma's endless jugs of custard
and tip
a blanket of yellow heaven upon their plate.'

We met in the middle between darkness and
hope,
I walked heavy, she as light
yet weighed equally in might.

A pivot
a moment
before the breaking out
breaking in
as if running in new shoes to unknown lands.
She moved as fast as I ran, I couldn't catch her and tomorrow
I'll fall further
in love, and in distance.

iii.
And there she reigns high
the Serpent of the skies.

Those below tilt upwards akin to faces of children being
cupped by her Mother hand, to wash the sleep from their
eyes.

Oh
how quickly we forget the winter of discontent when thawed
by your fingers on our skin.

Long nights of light,   with no need of me. No cry for my
shadow to loom too soon.

You linger beyond your prologue
shaking the stage into life and I can't help but
gaze. At the performance
from beneath the border of the horizon, from beneath the
weight of the soil,
as you toil to fill life with life once more. But soon

you'll yearn for me.

You'll thirst for my presence and my interlude will be noticed.
A Prelude to my Nocturne.
I may be the daughter of Chaos,
but I am your Mother.

Sahera Khan
My Glow

My glow.
It was exciting.
My tummy was beginning.
In time, my tummy started to mildly cramp.

I was concerned.

I contacted the clinic and they sent me to the hospital immediately.

There were a few communication barriers because of lockdown.

They scanned inside my tummy but my glow could not be found.

But it was still there.
So later, they scanned again.
Yes, the glow was there, like a pea.
Relieved!

My glow was growing but I was nausea.

Nervous for my first scan.

I saw the screen and I saw my tiny glow like a bean.
Amazing!

But my tiny glow was complicated.

I was sad and told the news only to my family.
I stayed positive and prayed to God.

I continued my health appointments;
the same cycle repeated: tests, scans, checks, and injections.

Of course, I must be careful with the virus around me and my glow.

My glow grew bigger – lots of movement in my tummy.

My final scan – scared.

My glow was not very well.
I was sad but prayed to God.
I went to the hospital urgently.

My glow couldn't reach full term.

I gave birth to a baby.

But I didn't hold my baby, because the doctors had to check their health.

I was blank, no emotions after a complicated birth.
They gave me my baby. I looked at him.
What a beautiful boy.

I smiled, cuddled, touched his hand and kissed his head.
I only had a couple of minutes with him.
He was taken to the care unit.
My heart was broken.

Pray to God that my baby will be coming home soon.
He is a beautiful baby.
Grateful to God.

My baby is my glow forever.

Lisa Kelly
Ear Trumpet

possibly used during a period of mourning, Europe, 1850-1910
Science Museum Group Collection

1.
In life she listened to me. Or at least tried.
Out of kindness, I raised my voice
to make her understand. Now I have died,
my dumb widow must mourn. My choice
of ear trumpet will be held to her deaf ear
with its ornate black lace collar and bow.
I warned on my death bed, Nothing to fear
if you occupy your hand with this gift I bestow.
She paled when I raised the spectre of the Workhouse,
reminded the sweet simpleton of the Institute for the Deaf.
Speech is a divine spark. My mute grey mouse
must listen for the ghost of her better half.

2.
Today, I stand naked as a sylph dressed in air.
He is under the ground and I float above his grave.
I frolic in front of a glass with the trumpet to my ear.
Its black lace bow looks dandy – this I will save,
rip it from its hard shaft and pin it to my curls.
The black lace collar will be food for the moths.
Look now at this denuded amplifying cone, its bare shell.
Let me fill it with cream to spill on mourning cloth,
or plant it in the heap of fresh earth that covers his bones,
cut a single white trumpet flower to place in its O.
It will bind him to his voice, as the north wind groans.
My hands are free to sign in their natural flow.

Bryony Parkes
Moving Words

Communication is visual
4D and constantly fluid
Words are moving pictures
Building scenes and images vivid
My head is home to a wonder
Of stories creatively described
Through glorious sign language
That is a treasure and treat for eyes
Compared to words being read
From a page standing linear
I bow to the superiority
Of what I see, not hear
Open your mind to imagination
Of stories told with flair
Via expert hands and expressions
That the whole body wears
Sentences don't exist
Words are not black and white
Instead exploring the beauty
Of rainbows, colour and light
Signs that have no words
Mean a richer portrayal
Complex and simple all at once
Ingredients for heart felt tales.

Time to be serious now
For society is seriously lacking
Information crucial for someone's health
Is missing in the planning
The prime minister and his peers
Need to wake up and see
The damage being done
To a valuable community
Sign language needs its place
Firmly rooted in society
Provision as a given
So herein is my plea
I ask you to respect
And meaningfully understand
The imperative that sign language
Should be equal across the land.

Sarah O Adedeji
Deaf Rights

to be amplified, not nullified,
and unified, with no room to divide;
to be front line, and not pushed aside
and fortified, not devitalised,
is all that we aspire to be
as we watch our people expire,
during our attempts to acquire
the rights that we so require
and the treatment that we desire;
but, also, rightfully deserve,
because, yes,
we may be small,
when in comparison to you all,
but, when it comes to our lives,
we will grow tall
and fight against all
that deem us too small
and unworthy of laws
that will give voice to our cause
and shine a light on us all
that have had to stay in thrall
to the voices of the world.

Liam O'Dell
The Home Secretary Doth Protest Too Much

A person commits an offence if [...] the person's act or omission causes serious harm to the public or a section of the public.

An act or omission causes serious harm to a person if, as a result, the person suffers [...] serious distress, serious annoyance [or] serious inconvenience.

The Police, Crime, Sentencing and Courts Bill, 2021.

To the Home Secretary, Ms Priti Patel.
This is my promise to fit within unspecified decibels,
to tame my frustrations to a controllable amount,
to squeeze #BeKind into a post on my Insta account,
to make requests to my oppressors with Ps and Qs,
not to get angry when they straight-out refuse;
to quietly whisper my complaints, and never cry or shout,
to 'keep calm and carry on' ignoring injustices that I'm pissed about,
to show passive compassion, and always be polite,
never rage through protests, civil disobedience or strikes;
to only partake in marches when your Government says it's alright,
most often when it defends the social values of the right.
Because change only happens when the progress is convenient,
despots despise growth, that's why the sentence isn't lenient,
ten years imprisonment for causing others irritation,
because nobody remembers protests full of exclamations.

All this law does is allow division to fester,
no media outcry when
cops
kettle
Black Lives Matter protesters.
statutes for statues.
If it's a demonstration against lockdown,
then you won't bat an eyelid,
but what really hits close to home, Secretary,
is when pointing out the climate crisis,
you use 'serious harm' to pick and choose your favourite voices,
turning the right-to-protest into your own personal choices,
creating an offence so individualistic and loosely defined,
it is you and the police who get to draw the line,
and we all know officers are great at understanding tone,
detaining members of a vigil, for a girl murdered walking home.
And I can't help but wonder,
would this law impact Pride?
It's always been a protest,
and I wouldn't be surprised,
if one homophobe, annoyed at us being proud,
ran to the police, saying that we're being too loud.
They'd have to take their word for it,
it's something which can't be measured –
prompting people to shut down protests,
for their own sadistic pleasure.

Those who complained
about 'cancel culture'
have everything to gain
from using this law to silence our pain.
You'll take our cardboard placards
and with them build
a box where our democracy,
our opinions, starve
under key and lock
So go ahead, Home Secretary,
take away our rights,
you'll just leave us hungry for change
and we've got quite the appetite.

Clare-Louise English
Pushing Boundaries

What is it about our boundaries that need them to be pushed?
What is it about our no's that invite them to be shhh'd?
Is this something they get taught at school,
some kind of fucking three times rule?

Push, 'No'
Push, 'No'
Push, 'oh for fuck's sake, fine'
Let's keep it nice, pour some more wine.

Or is it us getting the subliminal training?
Learning our choices all need re-framing?
Life's not a game show, we won't take your first answer,
we'll just keep pushing, till we get the right answer.

The answer we want, 'cos we've already decided
the choices in this exchange don't get divided.
Is it any wonder that we have to shout,
when all of our words are thrown into doubt.

Less of the chip chipping away at us
Less of the
      Drip
            Drip
And start by removing that entitlement chip.

No more softly, softly
No more being kind
Just so we're clear –
We know our own fucking mind.

John Wilson
The Dice Players

Nathaniel is looking forward to seeing what the fuss is about. He is an intensely self-conscious man, just shy of twenty-one years of age. Profoundly deaf from birth (never deaf and dumb, he is absolutely clear), he has never had any hearing. Most of his working day he spends in self-imposed isolation in the museum office.

He is already tired, even though it is only a Monday and only midday. Speaking is not easy. It is harder, more painful, for him to speak than it is to stay silent. His eyes smart from struggling to lipread people around him, but he hangs on to their words like a limpet: any scraps of information, even from grotesque lip movements or body language could be the word that saves him. People think that being deaf means you're stupid. Nathaniel knows this, but people who think like this are ignorant. They are the ones Nathaniel considers stupid.

He knows that today something is going on. There is a fuss. He can feel excitement in his office. He watches a discussion going on in the room.

And this is what he has managed to discover. First, a painting nobody knew existed, possibly a painting of great value, maybe even an Old Master, has been found in an attic, in a house just outside Middlesbrough, no distance at all from the office where they work.

Then another bit of information: someone took it away – he's not sure where, but it must have been to London – to be authenticated and restored. At last, it has come back home! Apparently, it travelled in the back of a Mini – which someone said was safer than an armoured personnel carrier. A strange thing to say, but Hearing people often say strange things.

So that's what the fuss is all about.

The discussion continues: the painting is back in Middlesbrough, on public display in an art gallery, about ten minutes away. Ah, now, some more information: the picture has already been exhibited, after it was restored, in Paris. The artist was French, someone people had forgotten about. They say the name. The first time Nathaniel misses it, but he concentrates, it looks like George something. He later discovers that it's Georges – Georges de La Tour – this is very exciting, because there are fewer than forty paintings by him still around.

At lunchtime Nathaniel slips out through the oak and glass doors of the copper-domed council museum. It is an old building, built for a sad reason, one Nathaniel always remembers. It was built by a grieving father as a memorial to his young son, whose life was snuffed out in the Boer War. Nathaniel thinks often about the young man who died all those years ago. He wonders what he was like.

When you have discovered something important, Nathaniel thinks, you need to find out about it for yourself. So, he walks briskly to the art gallery. He is keen to see what exactly his workmates were so excited about.

Someone catches his eye. Glancing back, it is a young man, dressed in cheap synthetic clothes. He is obviously gay, and is not ashamed if people know it. The young man licks his index finger, rubs it across the grimy slag path, and smears it on his eyelid. There are lots of grimy slag paths in this town. They go with steelmaking, and from a grimy path you can get eye-shadow. The young man likes to think of it as kohl.

Nathaniel is not unsusceptible to the charms of handsome young men. He feels a surge of admiration for him. People around here can be the most prejudiced in the world. Being deaf is perfect in this situation – he can be an observer, an outsider, engaged yet protected. Nathaniel watches the man saunter off, seemingly fulfilled in some way. Nathaniel wants to understand what it means to be fulfilled.

At the gallery, Nathaniel tiptoes through a couple of very white rooms. Finally, he comes to a dark room. He goes in and waits for his eyes to adjust to the dim light. As they do, he sees the single, solitary canvas, a glossy jewel-like luminescence shining through a veil of gleaming varnish.

It is an extraordinary picture. Four youthful soldiers, in a circle, playing dice by candlelight. A fifth man looks on. Nathaniel catches a glint of something particular in the painting which takes his breath away.

He steps back to get a fix on a huge white pearl earring, dangling from a beautifully feminine face. Nathaniel's first thought: is this a boy or a girl? Yes, a young man, now he can see. He is reminded of Vermeer's turbaned girl.

Nathaniel continues to scrutinise the painting. Why is he so moved by it? It is just an image of soldiers playing dice by candlelight. They are so far away from him in time, yet now, right here, in front of him.

Nathaniel peers at the label by the painting: *The Dice Players* – he hadn't picked up the title before. He looks back to consider it more carefully. The flame of a single candle is hidden by the sleeve of the only soldier wearing a helmet. The armour of the soldier in the middle reflects the glare of the flame. It brings up memories of the glow of the nearby steelworks.

The open hands show that dice, three of them, have been thrown. Nathaniel inches forward for a closer look. Each die had an ace on the top. Two men on the left are watching the game. One is an older man with shoulder-length hair, smoking a clay pipe; the other a young man resting his hands on the table, but Nathaniel continues to be entranced by the young man with the earring.

A couple of visitors appear at the entrance. Nathaniel's spell is broken.

There are times in his life which pass by, slipping away, leaving no trace in his mind. Others, however, etch deep marks into his memory, like carvings in stone. Sound plays no part in these memories, only what Nathaniel saw and experienced:

As a child, he was taught to speak whilst at oral deaf schools. It took an insufferably long time, and was tied up in anger, abuse, aggression, impatience, and contempt. A conglomeration that was based on the certainty that deafness and speech defects would be medically diagnosed and 'cured' by drinking bromide, wearing ill-fitting hearing aids, or enduring decades of Speech 'Therapy'. For Nathaniel and his deaf friends this was no different from putting people with mental health problems into straight-jackets. Too many teachers of the deaf had violated basic norms of decency when teaching deaf children.

Nathaniel returns his thoughts to the painting and its journey, which must have involved going to London. He has always dreamed of going there. It is the capital of freedom and self-expression, which he so yearns for, just as medieval knights searched for the Holy Grail. For Nathaniel, and possibly every lonesome deaf person, and for gay people too, London has a sense of community, identity and even more. There, he could truly be himself. He could be a boy with mascara – with Slag Path Kohl – on his eyes. Maybe he could even wear a pearl earring?

There and then, Nathaniel decides. He must move away, as far as he can go.

On an overcast September day Nathaniel boards the train from Darlington to London. He has no job now; just £100 in his pocket and a rucksack. It is not an unfamiliar journey. He endured it a thousand times for boarding school. He remembers the tug of homesickness, and peers through tearful eyes as the hills of his North hurtle past.

Those first days Nathaniel walks the streets of the West End, drinking in the sights of the city, theatres, cinemas, museums and shops. The pavements teem with humanity: tourists, office workers, children, drunkards and addicts. Nathaniel needs to keep his wits about him.

He has two lives, often in conflict. One, a wide community of deaf people who spend their leisure hours in the many deaf clubs and gathering places that only London can provide. The other, the deaf gay community. This group is isolated and usually lurks in the upstairs room of a pub, insulated from anti-gay attitudes in both hearing and deaf communities. It is a secret community in many ways, but it is here that Nathaniel is able to put on his mascara and pearl earring, and to be happy.

He stays, and makes a life for himself, becoming a histology technician in a pathology laboratory, where communication between him and his colleagues is kept to a mutually accepted minimum. All his life, he has felt like he didn't belong, and had got used to that sense of unbelonging.

But now he knows he can have something else.

One day Nathaniel is walking through Trafalgar Square. He sees that there is an exhibition of the work of Caravaggio and his contemporaries at the National Gallery. He ventures in. There are paintings of young men staring out with direct, almost provocative expressions.

But then something else: Nathaniel finds himself standing in front of an old friend. It is the *The Dice Players*. The five men are all still there, eternally absorbed in their game. He is taken back to the day when he made the most important decision of his life. The day the boy with the pearl earring told him to go to London – but the years have gone by, and even though that boy has not changed, Nathaniel has.

He looks again. He sees again the older man with the long hair smoking his clay pipe. He stands opposite the beautiful boy with the pearl earring. He seems to watch the younger men as if they are in danger. He has a wisdom which Nathaniel hadn't noticed before – he was too entranced by a beautiful face and a pearl earring.

Nathaniel smiles and wonders: if he was the boy with the pearl earring all those years ago, who is he now? Is it time to play a different role? This painting changed his life before and perhaps he needs to let it change him again.

He realises how much he belongs in this place, where he has grown older, and wiser. He has found the identity he was searching for.

Maryam Ebrahim
I Will Talk For You

O Mother,
O Father,
I will talk for you, so you are not ashamed,
I will talk for you, so you don't take the blame,
I will talk for you and continue with this game.

O Teacher,
O Teacher,
I will talk for you, so you can gaze with pride,
I will talk for you – a star in your mind's eye,
I will talk for you and continue with this lie.

O Doctor,
O Doctor,
I will talk for you, so you feel in the game,
I will talk for you, so you can stake a claim,
I will talk for you and continue with this charade.

But I ask all of you,
Before an encore from me
Stop.
Take a look –
Will you sign for me?

Lianne Herbert
Why Can't You Learn Sign Language?

my eyes *bleed* as i search
for clues on your lips and face
or in the sounds that i hear

my hands *ache* as i try to not
sign to you how i wish you would
to communicate with me

i'm growing *tired* of saying
the same thing that falls
on your deaf ears

why can't you learn sign language?

i'd *love* to have a conversation
with you with my eyes and hands
whilst you're still alive

i'd love us to get closer in
ways that don't rely on
sound

please, please, *please* could you learn?

if you *don't* or *can't*
i guess communication
with me is not
a priority

i've *asked* you nicely
plenty of times but
now i must keep
quiet as i know
you won't change

i *still* have a flicker
of hope that you will
and that's what
i'll try to hold onto

yours,

_____

Sarah O Adejeji
The Dancer

With eyes closed,
and body swaying,
the vibrations of the soundless music
travel through their spine,
to take residence in their mind.
on autopilot
arms
rise
and legs   go wide
as they think of a design
no, a story
no!
A movie,
to describe through the movement of limbs.

A pop to the chest flows into tutting arms
and consecutive waves waves waves
t-r-i-c-k-l-e into a body roll
that initiates a momentary krumping.
The dancer is led by the re**verb**erations of music –
the never-ending counts of eight [eight eight]
ticking in their brain.
Hearing doesn't come easy
as they glide across the space
letting emotions play across their face
– but feeling does.

Feeling is what they do best,
dancing through feeling
is the best thing they know.

They drop into a smooth side lunge
                    right elbow jutting out to the side.
and smile, head bobbing
   side   to   *side*
the move feels just right
perfectly in time
with the drum
and bass line.

Every twirl and every snap,
to the beat they always match.
Every lock
and every drop
is so in sync,
it makes your skin pop.
Every move causes you to be moved
every shudder causes hearts to stutter.
As the music ebbs to an end,
the dancer starts to descend,
and their leg they   e x t e n d
to a speaker that's their friend,
Just to catch that final blend.

Sarah O Adejeji
The Silent Linguist

hypnotising.

the way in which our hands flow as we sign is so beautiful,
that it can almost put you in a trance and, out of fear that
you will miss the subtle way our fingers move into positions
without breaking the fluidity, you remain mesmerised and
dare not to move your eyes, as if you've been hypnotised.

magical.

it was almost laughable that,
being silent is when we are the loudest
as our voices disappear automatically,
and our hands dance fanatically,
and our faces contort dramatically but,
actually, that's where the magic is.

entrancing.

one hand is the canvas, and the other, a pen.
many stories are written, and many drawings are painted.

one hand is the stage and the other the performer.
many dances are danced, and many songs are sung.

each creation is unique and is never a repeat.
so, every single piece is seen as a great feat.
it is artistic indeed and
many are left intrigued;
just entranced by the fact
that our voice is, in fact,
in the movements of our hands
and the recruitment of our limbs.

simple.

the fisting of a hand,
the swoop of a salute,
and the simple flutter of a finger
are all quick movements, pieced together
to create a short sequence in which
a question is asked:

your name what?

the simplicity of it all just leaves you in awe.

complex.

the shapes and the placements
are always the same
but the executions always differ,
and the sequences get longer,
but our hands never tire.

and the patterns that we string together
through the calculated actions of our fingers
and the messages that we deliver
even through the slightest of quivers
is enough of an emotional trigger
to send chills through your figure,

and the complexity of it all just leaves you in awe.

movement.

communicating through our hands,
and our eyes,
and even through our lips,
carries comfort which you can affix.

and communicating through our hands,
and our eyes,
and even through our lips,
is movement seen as
magic tricks
that only a few can unpick.

Marilyn Longstaff
Dreamcatcher
sometime between Christmas Day and New Year's Eve 2020

A strange gift from a Christian boss,
this dreamcatcher hangs above my bed.

I think of her every time I dust it.

It doesn't always work for the good,
captures dreams I'd rather not remember.

Last night, or somewhere in the early hours,

I dream a January holiday
with an unusual mix of poetry friends

in unsuitable cabins with few mod cons,

no curtains or doors on the ancient showers,
holes in the floor, inadequate heating.

Cabins, like us, that have seen better days.

Although they should be tethered to the ground,
I find myself in the naked shower, being towed to

God-knows-where, by some bloke in a Land Rover.

But, do you know what,
in these constricted times,

        I'd settle for that adventure.

Julie Boden
In Two Minds

My head, a bust of Janus, looks ahead and looks behind.
I'm vacillating, contemplating; can't make up my mind.

I'm hesitant... uncertain... I'm a little bit unclear.
If I jump out the frying pan – there's still a fire to fear.

And Robin isn't helping, sitting halfway up the stairs,
Can't go over, can't go under, he says, *when you're hunting bears.*

On my left shoulder's the devil; to my right the deep blue sea.
And somewhere, in the middle, there's an indecisive me

a-second-guess-your-second-guessing-kind-of-indecisive-me.

A squirrel's corpse cries, *I wish I'd decided to decide!*
The hedgehog, who curled up instead of running, well... he died.

I know that sitting on the fence is not the place to be

for this sort-of-second-guessing-kind-of-indecisive-me.

Some say, *Trust yourself to tea leaves, have a cup of Rosie Lee,*
Draw straws... get out the tarot cards... I Ching. That works for me,

or *I play paper-scissors-stone.* Yes, these things work for some,
while others roll out dice until prevarication's done.

But I'm stuck upon the fulcrum of this see-saw where I'll be

a-second-guess-your-second-guessing-kind-of-indecisive-me.

I set my chair to rise up; then I set it to recline.
Never fully sitting up or lying down, but I'll be fine

—for I can rest between the two—

I hope that you agree...
this kind of suits the second-guessing-indecisive-me.

Dee Cooke
De-stiffen

De-sit, from the hollow in the sofa you have made your own;
disrobe, and robe in comfort for the venture of the day.
Cast off all that for the last year you have only known;
sense the fresher cloth as you brave the friendly rays.

De-anchor, from the harbour of the clinging front door;
step, and step again, again, leave patterns with the sole.
Loosen each tiny joint as it lands on earth's miraculous floor;
breathe harder, as the million parts become the working whole.

Detach, once de-stiffened; bounce on awoken feet;
leave, for the briefest moment, the ground from where you come.
Shake the shadows from your bones and feel your warm heart beat;
wheel and windmill through the world: hurtle, fly, soar, run.

Sarah Clarke
This is Not a Race

Looking over the horizon
I take in the glistening blue sea
slightly tinged with green,
rays of the sun beaming
many boats lined up.
I turn my head, too
 many people bustling
on the harbour.

eyes closed I
try to imagine
the shuffling, the mingling,
many bodies together as one.
I open one eye, slowly
squinting,
straining to listen, so many voices,
I can't recognise the words.

Searching,
My mind in overdrive,
aware that people are rushing now.
What is happening?
People, singly, in twos and threes
climbing into their boats, shouting

'Time to go on the water!'
Thinking, *What is this contest?*

Boats small and tall, heavy and light,
Colours I have not observed before:
Crimson and cobalt and golden yellow.
Which will be the fastest?
That tall emerald one there, 51 on its sail?
Or this small, sleek bronze racer,
With number 2 on the side?

So many more craft
a variety of size, colour, shape.
I favour this black and white spotty one,
or that one there, number 44.
Maybe the orange striped yacht will be swift,
a lucky 7 or 9 on its mainsail?
What about this one just beside me
A simple rowing boat with a mighty 3 on its hull?

A horn sounds out as I gaze.
The boats start to move,
crews scramble to shift the oars,
start motors or turn the steering wheel,
all the boats in unison, manoeuvring into position.

I amble upon the crumbling stones
on the path beneath me,
watching, waiting, not understanding.

I trek further, wandering, meandering.
I spot someone in the distance,
using their hands, communicating.
Finally, I think, *someone to explain,
what exactly is going on.*
Although I think I know, still I hurry,

many vessels all going in one direction,
many shapes and sizes, an unfair race.
But where is the finish line?

I reach her, the signer; myself, breathless and excited,
Sweat seeping from my brow,
I watch her hands convey meaning,
Now I understand what is happening.
This. Is. Not. A. Race.
Oh! That explains why I couldn't see a finishing line,
and why all the boats are so different,
It is a life journey.

The boats progress
over the water
some fast, some slow
heading towards the other side.
This. Is. Not. A. Race?

A drip here, a drop there,
it starts to shower
mildly at first
then a torrent comes.

Soaking wet, we jostle
to find shelter
anywhere to get out of the downpour,
someplace where we can converse freely.

Her facial expressions, hands moving,
various hand-shapes explaining to me,
my eyebrows arching in wonder,
that's the beauty of the human race,

You are one of a kind,
I am me,
You are you.
we all move at our own pace.

This. Is. Not. A. Race.

Josephine Dickinson
La Favorite
After Couperin

Have you ever dreamt of falling
out of the sky?
with a violence as gentle
as gravity?

And was the gift you gave a river?
yet you received,
after falling without damage,
a thing as soft?

And your shape somehow remained the same
— passage paid —
a trajectory captured
out of the wind?

Were you eager to continue?
— to disappear?
in the smells and colours that you
lifted clear?

(Was it you who would embrace them,
or they you?
— you who in your sparring game
held the light?)

And, unstinting, hold a world
— for each —
you drove them from yet yourself wanted
to reach?

Was it there between earth's mantle
and the ground
you had your history, beginning
and end?

Or is it that you watch still for me, in dread or welcome?
— bravely —
ready to release a little music?
Then it was memory.

Terri Donovan
The Cycle (Of Important Nothings)
* indicates to go back to the previous star
– At the beginning of the line indicates a new person starts speaking
/ at the end of a line indicates to go straight to the next line.
This poem is to be spoken or signed, preferably by two people.

*–What happened?
–I wake up
–Then what?
–I walk down the stairs
(The stairs are yellow)
Dad... /
–Then what?
–I hear water,
Like an itch on raw skin /
–Then what?
–I walk down, along, the corridor
Wood (cold)
...Dad /
–Then what?
–I open the door
– And then?
– Her
Sink
Hunched over
Red
Cardi
–You smell?
–Oil
Gas

Washing up, Fairy you know
Egg
—You see?
—An attempt to /
—You see?
—Oil in soap water
Eggs open: Guts spewing
Frying pan: Other side!
—You say?
— it's 4am
—She?
—Breakfast
My (dead) name

—We?

—Hush
—I?

—Smooth the
Polyester red
Over her shoulders and
Back

—She?
—Looks,
just looks

sorry

It's nothing

Pass us
the frying pan,
Gran

Forehead kisses

Bed?

—

Yeah

hand
Hand

(Repeat)*

Khando Langri
First as Body, Then as Metaphor

A tree falls in the forest and I am
there to make sure no one hears it.
Beloved: It's not that I am
unwilling to be seized by sound,
every day, I am undone by
it.
There are no batteries small enough
for my hands, for the bee gently
drumming the glass pane with its body.

There is no classroom big enough
to contain my echoing valleys, the space
between the sighs of the boy who sits beside me.

Listen: I am a conch shell.
Waves crash and I am there
speaking
the language of the golden fish.

**Link to BSL videos
by the authors, and translators**
https://bit.ly/3BK0y3k

About Arachne Press

Arachne Press is a micro publisher of (award-winning!) short story and poetry anthologies and collections, novels including a Carnegie Medal nominated young adult novel, and a photographic portrait collection.
We are expanding our range all the time, but the short form is our first love. We keep fiction and poetry live, through readings, festivals (in particular our Solstice Shorts Festival), workshops, exhibitions and all things to do with writing.
https://arachnepress.com/

Follow us on Twitter:
@ArachnePress
@SolShorts

Like us on Facebook:
ArachnePress
SolsticeShorts2014

What Meets the Eye: the Deaf Perspective, is the second in a series of anthologies loosely linked by the theme of Maps and Mapping.

Already available *Where We Find Ourselves*
Coming soon:
Words from the Brink, Solstice Shorts 2021, Climate Crisis, Dec 2021
and
A470, Bilingual Poems for the Road, Mar 2022 (Welsh & English.)

Find out more about our authors at
https://arachnepress.com/writers/